Patricia Cornwell is a Senior Fellow at the International Crime Scene Academy at John Jay College of Criminal Justice, a founder of the Virginia Institute of Forensic Science and Medicine and a member of the Harvard-affiliated McLean Hospital's National Council, where she is an advocate for psychiatric research.

She is the 2008 winner of the Galaxy British Book Awards' Books Direct Crime Thriller of the Year – the first American ever to win this prestigious award. Her most recent number one bestsellers include *Book of the Dead*, *At Risk* and *Portrait of a Killer: Jack the Ripper – Case Closed*. Her earlier works include *Post-mortem* – the only novel to win five major crime awards in a single year – and *Cruel and Unusual*, which won the coveted Gold Dagger Award in 1993.

Visit the author's website at www.patriciacornwell.com

Also by Patricia Cornwell

THE SCARPETTA NOVELS

Postmortem
Body of Evidence
All That Remains
Cruel and Unusual
The Body Farm
From Potter's Field
Cause of Death
Unnatural Exposure
Point of Origin
Black Notice
The Last Precinct
Blow Fly
Trace
Predator
Book of the Dead

ANDY BRAZIL SERIES

Hornet's Nest
Southern Cross
Isle of Dogs

OTHER FICTION

At Risk

NON-FICTION

Portrait of a Killer: Jack the Ripper – Case Closed

BIOGRAPHY

Ruth, a Portrait: The Story of Ruth Bell Graham

OTHER WORKS

Food to Die For: Secrets from Kay Scarpetta's Kitchen
Life's Little Fable
Scarpetta's Winter Table

THE FRONT

PATRICIA CORNWELL

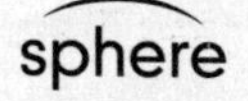

SPHERE

First published in the United States in 2008 by G.P. Putnam's Sons,
a division of Penguin Group (USA) Inc.
First published in Great Britain in 2008 by Little, Brown
This paperback edition published in 2008 by Sphere
Reprinted 2008

A CIP catalogue record for this book
is available from the British Library.

ISBN 978-0-7515-3965-3

Typeset in Caslon by M Rules
Printed and bound in Great Britain by
Clays Ltd, St Ives plc

Papers used by Sphere are natural, renewable and recyclable products sourced from well-managed forests and certified in accordance with the rules of the Forest Stewardship Council.

Mixed Sources
Product group from well-managed
forests and other controlled sources
www.fsc.org Cert no. SGS-COC-004081
© 1996 Forest Stewardship Council

Sphere
An imprint of
Little, Brown Book Group
100 Victoria Embankment
London EC4Y 0DY

An Hachette Livre UK Company
www.hachettelivre.co.uk

www.littlebrown.co.uk

TO URSULA MACKENZIE,

who publishes me so brilliantly in the UK.

1

Win Garano sets two lattes on a picnic table in front of the John F. Kennedy School of Government. It's a sunny afternoon, mid-May, and Harvard Square is crowded. He straddles a bench, overdressed and sweaty in a black Armani suit and black patent-leather Prada shoes, pretty sure the original owner of them is dead.

He got a feeling about it when the saleslady in the Hand-Me-Ups shop said he could have the "gently worn" outfit for ninety-nine dollars. Next she pulled out suits, shoes, belts, ties, even socks. DKNY, Hugo Boss, Gucci, Hermès, Ralph

Lauren. All from the same *celebrity whose name I can't tell you,* and it occurred to Win that not so long ago, a wide receiver for the Patriots got killed in a car wreck. One eighty, six feet tall, muscular but not a moose. In other words, about Win's size.

He sits alone at the picnic table, more self-conscious by the moment. Students, faculty, the elite—most of them in jeans, shorts, carrying knapsacks—cluster at other tables, deep in conversations that include very few comments about the dull lecture District Attorney Monique Lamont just gave at the Forum. *No Neighbor Left Behind.* Win warned her it was a confusing title, not to mention a banal topic for such a prestigious political venue. She's not going to appreciate that he was right. He doesn't appreciate that she ordered him here on his day off so she could boss him around, belittle him. Make a note of this. Make a note of that. Call so and so. Get her a coffee. Starbucks. Latte with skim milk and Splenda. Wait for her outside in the heat while she hobnobs inside the air-conditioned Littauer Center.

He sullenly watches her emerge from the brick building, escorted by two plainclothes officers from the Massachusetts State Police, where Win is a homicide investigator currently assigned to the Middlesex County District Attorney's detective unit. In other words, assigned to Lamont, who called him at home last night and said effective immediately, he's on leave from his regular duties. *I'll explain after my lecture at the Forum. See you at two.* No further details.

She pauses to give an interview to the local ABC affiliate, then to NPR. She talks with reporters from *The Boston Globe,* the AP, and that Harvard student, Cal Tradd, who writes for the *Crimson,* thinks he's from *The Washington Post.* The press loves Lamont. The press loves to hate her. No one is indifferent to the powerful, beautiful DA—today, conspicuous in a bright green suit. Escada. This year's spring collection. Seems she's been on quite the shopping spree of late, a new outfit practically every time Win sees her.

She continues talking to Cal as she walks confidently across the brick plaza, past massive planters of azaleas, rhododendrons, and pink and white dogwoods. Blond, blue-eyed, pretty-boy Cal, so cool and collected, so sure of himself, never flustered, never frowns, always so damn pleasant. Says something while scribbling on his notepad, and Lamont nods, and he says something else, and she keeps nodding. Win wishes the guy would do something stupid, get himself kicked out of Harvard. Flunking out would be even better. What a friggin' pest.

Lamont dismisses Cal, signals for her plain-clothes protection to give her privacy, and sits across from Win, her eyes hidden by reflective gray-tinted glasses.

"I thought it went well." She picks up her latte without thanking him for it.

"Not much of a turnout. But you seemed to make your point," he says.

"Obviously, most people, including you, don't grasp the enormity of the problem." That flat tone she uses when her narcissism has been insulted. "The decline of neighborhoods is potentially as destructive as global warming. Citizens have no respect for law enforcement, no interest whatsoever in helping us or each other. This past weekend I was in New York, walking through Central Park, and noticed a backpack abandoned on a bench. Do you think a single person thought to call the police? Maybe consider there could be an explosive device inside it? No. Everyone just kept going, figuring if it blew up, it wasn't their problem as long as they didn't get hurt, I suppose."

"The world's going to hell, Monique."

"People have slipped into complacency, and here's what we're going to do about it," she says. "I've set the stage. Now we create the drama."

Every day with Lamont is a drama.

She toys with her latte, looks around to see who's looking at her. "How do we get attention? How do we take people who are jaded, desensitized, and make them care about crime? Care so much they decide to get involved at a grassroots level? Can't be gangs, drugs, carjackings, robberies, burglaries. Why? Because people want a crime problem that's, let's be honest, front-page news but happens to others, not to them."

"I wasn't aware people actually want a crime problem."

He notices a skinny young woman with kinky red hair loitering near a Japanese maple not far from them. Dressed like Raggedy Ann, right down to her striped stockings and clunky shoes. Saw her the other week, in downtown Cambridge, loitering around the courthouse, probably waiting to go before a judge. Probably some petty crime like shoplifting.

"An unsolved sexual homicide," Lamont is saying. "April fourth, 1962, Watertown."

"I see. Not a cold case this time but a frozen one," he says, keeping his eye on Raggedy Ann. "I'm surprised you even know where Watertown is."

In Middlesex County, her jurisdiction—along with some sixty other modest municipalities she doesn't give a damn about.

"Four square miles, population thirty-five thousand, very diverse ethnic base," she says. "The perfect crime that just so happens to have been committed in the perfect microcosm for my initiative. The chief will partner you up with his lead detective . . . You know, the one who drives that monstrous crime scene truck. Oh, what is it they call her?"

"Stump."

"That's right. Because she's short and fat."

"She has a prosthesis, a below-the-knee amputation," he says.

"Cops can be so insensitive. I believe the two of you know each other, from the little grocery store around the corner where she works a second job. So that's a good start. Helps to be friends with someone you're going to spend a lot of time with."

"It's an upscale gourmet shop, and isn't just a second job, and we're not friends."

"You sound defensive. The two of you go out, maybe not get along? Because that could be a problem."

"Nothing personal between us, never even worked a case with her," Win says. "But I would think you have, since Watertown has plenty of crime and she's been around as long as you have."

"Why? Has she talked about me?"

"Usually we talk about cheese."

Lamont glances at her watch. "Let's get to the facts of the case. Janie Brolin."

"Never heard of her."

"British. She was blind, decided to spend a year in the States, chose Watertown, most likely because of Perkins, probably the most famous school for the blind in the world. Where Helen Keller went."

"Perkins wasn't located in Watertown back in the Helen Keller days. It was in Boston."

"And why would you know trivia like that?"

"Because I'm a trivial person. And obviously you've been planning this *drama* for a while. So why did you wait until the last minute to tell me about it?"

"This is very sensitive and must be handled very discreetly. Imagine being blind and realizing there's an intruder inside your apartment. That horror factor and something far more important. I think you're going to discover she very well may have been the Boston Strangler's first victim."

"You said early April 1962?" Win frowns. "His alleged first murder wasn't until two months later, in June."

"Doesn't mean he hadn't killed before, just that earlier cases weren't linked to him."

"How do you propose we prove the Janie Brolin murder—or the Strangler's other thirteen alleged murders, for that matter—was committed by him when we still don't really know who he was?"

"We have Albert DeSalvo's DNA."

"No one's ever proved he was the Strangler, and more to the point, do we have DNA from the Janie Brolin case for comparison?"

"That's for you to find out."

He can tell by her demeanor there's no DNA and she damn well knows it. Why would there be, some forty-five years later? Back then, there was no such thing as forensic DNA or even a thought that there might be someday. So forget proving or disproving anything, as far as he's concerned.

"It's never too late for justice," Lamont pontificates—or Lamonticates, as he calls it. "It's time to unite citizens and police in fighting crime. To take back our neighborhoods, not just here but worldwide." Same thing she just said in her uninspiring lecture. "We're going to create a model that will be studied everywhere."

Raggedy Ann is sending text messages on her cell phone. What a whack job. Harvard Square's full of them. The other day, Win saw some guy licking the sidewalk in front of the Coop.

"Obviously, nothing about this to the press until the case is solved. Then, of course, it comes from me. It's too hot for May," she complains, getting up from the picnic table. "Watertown tomorrow morning, ten sharp, the chief's office."

She leaves her barely touched latte for him to dutifully toss in the trash.

An hour later, Win is finishing his third rep on the leg press when his iPhone vibrates like a large insect. He picks it up, wipes his face with a towel, puts on the wireless earpiece.

"Sorry. You're on your own," Stump says, in response to the voice mail he left her.

"We'll talk later." He has no intention of discussing it in the middle of the Charles Hotel health spa, which he can't afford but is allowed to use in exchange for his security expertise and connections.

In the locker room, he takes a quick shower, changes back into his same outfit except for his shoes, which he swaps out for motorcycle boots. He grabs his helmet, his armored mesh jacket, and gloves. His motorcycle is parked in front of the hotel, a red Ducati Monster, protected by traffic cones, in his reserved spot on the sidewalk. He's tucking his gym bag inside the hard case, locking it, when Cal Tradd walks up.

Cal says, "I figured a guy like you would ride the Superbike."

"Really? Why would you figure that?" Before he can catch himself.

The last thing he wants is to engage the spoiled little bastard, but he's knocked off balance, would never have guessed Cal would know anything about motorcycles, certainly not a Ducati 1098 S Superbike.

"Always wanted one," Cal says. "Ducati, Moto Guzzi, Ghezzi-Brian. But you start piano lessons when you're five, forget even a skateboard."

Win's sick and tired of the reminder. The mini Mozart, giving recitals by the time he was five.

"So when are we going to ride around together?" Cal goes on.

"What's so hard about the words *no* or *never*? I don't have ridealongs and I hate publicity. And I've told you this . . . let's see. About fifty times now?"

Cal digs in a pocket of his khakis, pulls out a folded piece of paper, hands it to him. "My numbers. Same ones you probably threw away last time

I gave them to you. Maybe you'll call me, give me a chance. Just like Monique said in her lecture. Cops and the community need to work together. There's a lot of bad stuff going on out there."

Win walks off without so much as a *see you later*, heads toward Pittinelli's Gourmet Market, another place he can't afford. It took some nerve to wander in a couple months ago, see if he could work out an arrangement with Stump, who he'd heard of but never met. They aren't friends, probably don't even get along, but have a mutually beneficial arrangement. She gives him discounts because he happens to be state police and happens to be headquartered in Cambridge, where her market is located. Put it this way, it just so happens that Cambridge cops no longer ticket Pittinelli's delivery trucks when they're in violation of ten-minute parking zones.

He opens the front door and runs into Raggedy Ann, on her way out, tossing an empty Fresca can into a trash bin. The freako acts as if she doesn't see him, the same way she did a little while ago at the School of Government. Now that he thinks of it, she treated him as if he were invisible the other week, too, when she was hanging around the courthouse, and he passed within inches of her, even said "excuse me." Close up, she smells like baby powder. Maybe it's all the makeup she's wearing.

"What's going on?" he says, blocking her way. "Seems like we keep running into each other."

She pushes past him, hurrying along the busy sidewalk, cuts through an alleyway. Gone.

Stump is stocking shelves with olive oil, the air pungent with the aroma of imported cheeses, prosciutto, salami. Some college kid is sitting behind the counter, lost in a paperback, the shop otherwise empty.

"What's with Raggedy Ann?" Win asks.

Stump looks up from her crouched position in the aisle, hands him a corked bottle shaped like a flask. "Frantoio Gaziello. Unfiltered, a little grassy, with a hint of avocado. You'll love it."

"She was just in your shop? And right before that, she was hanging around Lamont and me at the School of Government. And I've seen her around the courthouse, too. A little coincidental, maybe?" He studies the bottle of olive oil, looking for the price. "Maybe she's stalking me."

"I certainly would if I were some pitiful, deranged street person who thinks she's a rag doll. Probably from one of the local shelters," Stump says. "In and out, never buys anything except Fresca."

"Sure drank it fast. Unless she didn't finish it. Tossed the can in the trash as she was coming out of your store."

"Her MO. Looks around, drinks her Fresca, and leaves. Seems harmless."

"Well, she's starting to give me a creepy feeling. What's her name, and which shelter? I think it would be a good idea to run a background on her."

"I don't know anything about her except she's not right." Twirling her finger at her temple.

"So, how long you known about Lamont's assigning me to Watertown?"

"Let me see." She looks at her watch. "You left your voice mail an hour and a half ago? Let me do the math. I've known for an hour and a half."

"That's what I thought. Nobody's told you, so she makes sure from the get-go that you and I don't get along."

"I don't need some harebrained new hobby right

now. She sends you to Watertown on some secret mission, don't come crying to me."

He crouches next to her. "You ever heard of the Janie Brolin case?"

"You can't grow up in Watertown and not have heard of that case, which was half a friggin' century ago. Your DA's nothing but a consummate, cold-blooded politician."

"She's your DA, too, unless Watertown PD's seceded from Middlesex County."

"Look," she says, "it's not my problem. I don't give a damn what she and the chief have cooked up. I'm not doing it."

"Since it occurred in Watertown, since there's no statute of limitations for homicides, technically it is your problem if the case is reopened. And as of now, looks like it has been."

"Technically, homicides in Massachusetts, with rare exception, such as Boston, are the jurisdiction of the state police. Certainly you guys remind us of that on a regular basis when you show up at the scene, take over the investigation, even if you don't know a damn thing about anything. Sorry, you're on your own."

"Come on, Stump. Don't be like this."

"We just had another bank robbery this morning." Arranging bottles on shelves. "Fourth in three weeks. Plus the hair salon breaks, car breaks, house breaks, copper thefts, hate crimes. Never stops. I'm a little busy for cases that happened before I was born."

"Same bank robber?"

"Same-o, same-o. Hands the teller a note, empties the cash drawer, call goes out over BAPERN."

Boston Area Police Emergency Radio Network. So local cops can talk to one another, assist one another.

"Meaning every cop car on the planet shows up, lights and sirens full-tilt. All of downtown looks like a Christmas parade. Ensuring our one-man Bonnie and Clyde knows exactly where we are so he can stay out of sight until we're gone," she says as a customer walks in.

"How much?" Win refers to the bottle of olive oil he's still holding.

More customers. Almost five p.m., and people are getting off work. Pretty soon, it will be standing room only. Stump sure as hell isn't a cop for the money, and he's never figured out why she doesn't retire from the department and have a life.

"It's yours at cost." She gets up, walks to another aisle, picks out a bottle of wine, gives it to him. "Just got it in. Tell me what you think."

A 2002 Wolf Hill pinot noir. "Sure," he says. "Thanks. But why the sudden kill-me-with-kindness act?"

"Giving you my condolences. Must be fatal working for her."

"While you're feeling sorry for me, mind if I get a few pounds of Swiss, cheddar, Asiago, roast beef, turkey, wild rice salad, baguettes? And kosher salt, five pounds would be great."

"Jesus. What the hell do you do with that stuff? Throw margarita parties for half of Boston?" As she stands up, so at ease with her prosthesis, he rarely remembers she has one. "Come on. Since I feel so sorry for you, I'll buy you a drink," she says. "One cop to another, let me give you a little advice."

They collect empty boxes and carry them to the storeroom in back, and she opens the walk-in refrigerator, grabs two diet cream sodas, and says, "What you need to focus on is motive."

"The killer's?" Win says, as they sit at a folding table, walled in by cases of wine, olive oils, vinegars, mustards, chocolates.

"Lamont's."

"You must have worked a lot of cases with her over the years, but she acts as if the two of you have never met," he says.

"Bet she does. I don't guess she told you about the night we got so ripped, she had to sleep on my couch."

"No way. She doesn't even socialize with cops, much less get drunk with them."

"Before your time," says Stump, who's older than Win by at least five years. "Back in the good ole days before an alien took over her body, she was a kick-ass prosecutor, used to show up at crime scenes, hang out with us. One night after a murder-suicide, the two of us ended up at Sacco's, started drinking wine, got so wasted we left our cars and walked to my place. Like I said, she ended up spending the night. We were so hungover the next day, both of us called in sick."

"You must be talking about someone else." Win can't envision it, has a weird feeling in the pit of his stomach. "You sure it wasn't some other assistant DA, and maybe over the years you've gotten the two of them confused?"

Stump laughs, says, "What? I've got Alzheimer's? Unfortunately, the Lamont you know never goes to crime scenes unless television trucks are everywhere, hardly ever sees a courtroom, has nothing to do with cops unless she's giving them orders, and doesn't care about criminal justice anymore, only power. The Lamont I knew may have had an ego, but why wouldn't she? Harvard Law, beautiful, smart as hell. But decent."

"She and *decent* don't know each other." He doesn't understand why he's suddenly so angry and territorial, and before he can stop himself, he nastily adds, "Sounds like you have a slight touch of the Walter Mitty syndrome. Maybe you've been a lot of different people in life, because the person I'm drinking a cream soda with is short and fat, according to Lamont."

Only thing short about Stump is her dark hair. And she's certainly not fat. In fact, now that he's paying attention, he has to say she's pretty damn buff, must work out a lot, has a great body, actually. Not bad looking. Well, maybe a little masculine.

"I'd appreciate it if you didn't stare at my chest," she says. "Nothing personal. I tell all the men that when I'm alone with them in the back of the shop."

"Don't assume I'm hitting on you," he says. "Nothing personal. I tell all the women that when I'm alone with them. Tell men, too, if the need arises. So to speak."

"Had no idea you were such a cocky dude. So to speak. Arrogant, for sure. But wow." She looks intently at him. Sips her soda.

Green eyes with flecks of gold in them. Nice teeth. Sensuous lips. Well, a little wrinkled.

"And here's another house rule," she says. "I have two legs."

"Goddamn. I haven't said a thing about your leg."

"That's my point. I don't have *a leg.* I have two. And I've seen you checking."

"If you don't want to draw attention to your prosthesis, then why do you call yourself Stump? For that matter, why do you put up with anybody calling you Stump?"

"I don't guess it might occur to you that I was called Stump before I had a bad day on my motorcycle."

He doesn't say anything.

"Since you're a biker boy, let me give you a tip," she says. "Try not to let some redneck in a pickup truck run you into a guardrail."

Win suddenly remembers his soda. Takes a swallow.

"And another word tip?" She tosses her empty can into a trash bin that's a good twenty feet away. "Stay away from literary allusions. I taught English lit before I decided to be a cop. Walter Mitty wasn't a lot of different people, he was a daydreamer."

"Why the nickname, if it's not about your leg? You've got me curious."

"Why Watertown? That's what you should be curious about."

"Obviously, because the murder occurred there," he says. "Maybe because Lamont knows you—even if she acts like she doesn't. Or at least she used to know you. Before you got short and fat."

"She can't stand that I saw her drunk, and know a lot about her because of what happened that night. Forget it. She didn't pick Watertown because of the case. She picked the case because of Watertown."

"She picked the case because it isn't just any old unsolved murder," Win retorts. "Unfortunately, it's one the media will love. A blind woman visiting from the UK is sexually assaulted and murdered . . ."

"No question Lamont will milk it for all it's worth. But it's worth more than one thing. She has other agendas."

"Always does."

"It's also about the FRONT," Stump says.

Friends, Resources, Officers Networking Together.

"In the last month, five more departments joined our coalition," she goes on. "We're up to sixty, have access to K-nine, SWAT, antiterrorism, crime scene investigation, and most recently a helicopter. We're still making bricks without straw, but we're on our way to needing less and less from the state police."

"Which I think is great."

"The hell you do. State police hates the FRONT. Lamont most of all hates the FRONT, and what a coincidence. It's headquartered in Watertown. So she's siccing you on us, setting us up to look like the Keystone Kops. We have to have some superhero state police investigator come in and save the day so Lamont can remind everyone how important the state police is and why it should get all the support and funding. A wonderful bonus is she gets back at me, makes me look bad, because she'll never forgive me for what I know."

"What you know?"

"About her." It's obvious that's all Stump intends to say about it.

"I don't understand how our solving your old case makes you look bad."

"*Our* solving it? *Unh-uh.* I keep telling you. You're on your own."

"And you wonder why the state police doesn't like . . . Hell, never mind."

She leans forward, meets his eyes, says, "I'm warning you, and you're not listening. She'll make sure the FRONT looks bad whether the case is solved or not. You're being used in ways you don't even know. Being set up in ways you can't even imagine. But start with this: The FRONT gets big enough one of these days? Then what? Maybe you guys don't get to be bullies anymore."

"We're bound by state law just like you are," Win says. "It's not about bullying, and you'll never hear me say the system's fair."

"Fair? How about worst conflict of interests in the entire United States? You guys have complete control over all homicide investigations. Your labs process all evidence. Even the damn death investigators at the morgue are state police. And then the DA whose state police investigative unit works all this, soup to nuts, is the one who prosecutes the case. For you and yours truly here, that would be Lamont, who answers to the Attorney General, who answers to the governor. Meaning the governor de facto has control over all homicide investigations in Massachusetts. You're not dragging me into this. It's headed only one way—toward disaster."

"Doesn't appear your chief thinks so."

"Doesn't matter what he thinks. He has to do what she says. And he won't take the blame, will just pass it down the line. Trust me," Stump says, "get out while you can."

2

Lamont used her reelection last fall as an excuse to fire every member of her staff. Fresh starts are a compulsion of hers. Especially when it comes to people. Once they serve their useful purpose it's time for change, or, as she puts it, a *resurrection* from something that's no longer vital.

Although she doesn't waste energy on personal reflection, a remote part of her is aware that her inability to maintain long-term relationships might not serve her well as she ages. Her father, for example, was extraordinarily successful, handsome, and charming but died completely alone in Paris last year, his body not found for days. When Lamont went through his belongings, she discovered years of birthday and holiday gifts he'd never opened, including a number of expensive pieces of art glass from her. Explaining why he never bothered to have his secretary call or dictate a thank-you note.

The Middlesex County courthouse is a concrete-and-brick high-rise in the dreary, crime-ridden heart of Cambridge's government center, her office on the second floor. As she steps off the elevator and notices the detective unit's closed door, her internal weather turns overcast. Win won't be inside his cubicle anymore, not for God knows how long. His reassignment to Watertown will make it difficult for her to demand his presence whenever she pleases.

"What is it?" she asks, when she finds her press secretary, Mick, sitting on the sofa in her corner office, talking on his phone.

She makes her usual cutthroat motion, indicating for him to end the call instantly. And he does.

"Don't tell me there's a problem. I'm in no mood for problems," she says.

"We have a little situation," says Mick, still new at the job, but promising.

He's handsome, polished, shows well, and does what he's told. She settles behind her glass desk inside her glass-filled office. Her ice palace, as Win calls it.

"If the situation's *little,* you wouldn't be in my office, waiting to pounce on me the instant I walk in," she says.

"I'm sorry. I'm not going to say I told you so . . ."

"You just did."

"I've been quite vocal about what I think of your reporter friend."

He means Cal Tradd. Lamont doesn't want to hear it.

"Let me find a way to say this delicately," Mick says.

It takes a lot to unnerve her, but she knows the warning signs. A tightness in her chest, a chilly breath on the back of her neck, an interruption in the normal steady rhythm of her heart.

"What has he said to you?" she asks.

"I'm more concerned about what you've said to him. Did you do something to make him spiteful?" Mike says bluntly.

"What the hell are you talking about?"

"Maybe you slighted him in some way. Such as giving that front-page story to the *Globe* last month instead of to him."

"Why would I give him a front-page anything? He works for a student newspaper."

"Well, can you think of any other reason he might have to get you back for something?"

"People never seem to need a reason."

"YouTube. Just posted a few hours ago. Frankly, I don't know what we're going to do about it."

"Do about what? And your job is to always know what to do about it—whatever it is," she retorts.

Mick gets up from the sofa, moves next to her, commandeers her computer, and logs on to the Internet, on to YouTube.

A video clip.

Carly Simon's "You're So Vain" as Lamont walks into a ladies' room, stops at a sink, opens her ostrich-skin handbag. Begins touching up her makeup in the mirror, primping, studying every angle of her face, her figure, experimenting with buttons on her blouse, which to button, which to unbutton. Pulling up her skirt, adjusting her panty-hose. Opening her mouth wide, examining her teeth. A voiceover from her own reelection campaign reciting "Clamping Down On Crime. Monique Lamont, DA for Middlesex County."

Instead of a handcuff snapping shut at the end of the ad, her teeth in the mirror do.

"Is this why you brought up Cal?" Severely. "Immediately assuming he's to blame? Based on what?"

"He's your shadow, practically stalks you. He's immature. It's something a college kid would do . . ."

"Such a strong case you make." Sarcastically. "Good thing I'm the DA, not you."

Mike stares at her, wide-eyed. "You're going to defend him?"

"He couldn't possibly have done it," she says. "Whoever recorded this clearly was in the ladies' room. A female, in other words."

"And it would be easy enough for him to pass as a damn girl . . ."

"Mick. He follows me like a puppy, was hanging around me the entire time I was at the School of Government. He had no time to suddenly become a cross-dresser or hide in the damn ladies' room."

"I didn't realize—"

"Of course you didn't. You weren't there. But you're right. The first order of business always is to find out who betrayed me." Pacing. "Most likely, some female student in a stall saw me through a crack in the door and recorded all this nonsense with her cell phone. The price of being a public figure. No one will take it seriously."

Mick stares at her as if she just fell off a shelf and shattered—like one of her pieces of art glass.

"Further," she says, "what matters is whether you look good. And I'm happy to say, I do." She replays the clip, reassured by her exotically beautiful face and perfect teeth, her shapely legs, her enviable bosom. "Make a note of it, Mick. That's how it works out there."

"Not exactly," he says. "The governor called."

She stops pacing. The governor never calls.

"About YouTube," Mick says. "He wants to know who's behind it."

"Let me see. I must have it written down somewhere."

"Well, it's an embarrassment no matter who did it. And when you look bad, he looks bad, since he's the one who . . ."

"What did he say, exactly?" she asks.

"I didn't talk to him directly."

"Of course you didn't talk to him directly." Angrily pacing again. "Nobody talks to him directly."

"Not even you." As if she needs to be reminded. "And after all you did for him," Mick adds. "You haven't seen him once. He never returns your phone calls . . ."

"This might be our opportunity." She cuts him off yet again, her thoughts like pool balls, scattering across the felt, clacking into pockets. "Yes. Absolutely. The best revenge is success. So what do we do? We turn this YouTube debacle to my advantage. My chance to have an audience with His Highness and get his support for my new crime initiative. He'll be interested when he sees what's in it for him."

She instructs Mick to get the governor's chief of staff on the phone. Now. It's urgent she sit down with Governor Howard Mather immediately. Mick suggests she might have to "grovel," and she reminds him never to use that word unless he's talking about someone else. However, she concedes, if she finally acknowledges Mather as her mentor, that will have an impact. She really needs his advice. She's suddenly found herself in a PR nightmare. She fears it could reflect poorly on him and doesn't know what to do. Et cetera.

"That will be hard for him to resist," she adds.

"But what if he does? Then what do I do?"

"Stop asking me to do your job!" she erupts.

In a very different part of Cambridge is the rundown frame house where Win was raised by his grandmother, Nana. Overwhelmed by ivy, flowering shrubs, and trees, her yard has become a subdivision of bird- and bat houses, and feeders.

His motorcycle bumps and fishtails over the rutted, unpaved driveway, and he parks near Nana's ancient Buick. Helmet off, and his ears are filled with the fairylike music of wind chimes stirred by the breeze, as if magical sprites alight on trees and the eaves of Nana's home and decide not to leave. She says they drive off mean and niggling entities, which should include the neighbors, Win thinks. Selfish, bigoted, rude. Fighting over shared driveways and off-street parking. Staring suspiciously at the steady stream of people who show up at the house.

He pops the trunk of the old Buick, which of course Nana hasn't bothered to lock, places his motorcycle gear inside, opens her back door, steps over the line of kosher salt on the floor. She's sitting in her kitchen, busy laminating bay laurel leaves in wide strips of transparent tape, the TV tuned to a classical music station. Miss Dog—deaf and blind and technically stolen because Win sneaked her away from her abusive owner—is under the table, snoring.

He sets his gym bag on the kitchen counter, then a knapsack filled with groceries, leans down, kisses Nana's cheek, says, "As usual, your car wasn't locked. Your door wasn't locked, and your alarm isn't set."

"My darling boy." Her eyes are bright, her long, snowy hair piled on top of her head. "Tell me about your day."

He opens the refrigerator, the cupboards, putting away her groceries, says, "Bay leaves don't deter burglars. That's why you have an alarm system and good locks. You at least locking up and setting the alarm at night?"

"Nobody's interested in an old woman who has nothing worth stealing. Besides, I have all the protection I need."

He sighs, does no good to nag her, pulls out a chair, rests his hands in his lap because there's no room on the table for them, virtually every inch occupied by crystals, candles, statues, icons, talismans, or lucky charms. She hands him two large laminated bay leaves, her silver jewelry clinking, a ring on every finger, bracelets up to her elbows.

"Put these in your boots, my darling," she tells him. "One in the left, one in the right. Don't do like you did last time."

"What might that have been?" He slips the laminated leaves in his pocket.

"You didn't put them in your shoes, and what did the Husk do?"

What she calls Lamont. An empty shell, nothing there.

"She gave you some awful job. A dangerous one," Nana says. "Laurel is the herb of Apollo. When you wear it in your shoes, your boots, you stand on victory. Make sure the tip points toward the toe, the stem toward the heel."

"Yeah, well, I just got another awful job."

"Full of lies," Nana says. "Be careful what you do, because it isn't about what she says."

"I know what it's about. Ambition. Selfishness. Hypocrisy. Vanity. Persecuting me."

Nana cuts off another strip of tape. "Justice is what I need in thought, word, and deed. I'm seeing a revolving sign and rubber marks on pavement. Skid marks. What's that about?"

He thinks of Stump's motorcycle accident, says, "Got no idea."

"Be very careful, my darling. Especially on your motorcycle. I wish you wouldn't ride that thing." Laminating another bay leaf.

When the price of gas hit three dollars a gallon, he sold his Hummer and bought the Ducati. Then what a coincidence. About a week later, Lamont came up with a new policy: Only her investigators on call could take home their state police cars.

"For tonight anyway, you get your wish because I need to fill your old battleship with gas," he says to

Nana. "Will bring it back tomorrow. Even though you've got no business behind the wheel."

He can't stop her. So at least he'll make sure she doesn't end up stranded on the roadside somewhere. Nana tends to forget about flat-footed realities, such as keeping her car filled with gas, checking the oil, making sure her registration is in the glove box, locking her doors, buying groceries, paying bills. Little things like that.

"Your clothes will be nice and clean. As always, my darling." Indicating his gym bag on the kitchen counter. "What touches your skin and the magic begins."

Indulging her in another one of her rituals. She insists on hand-washing his workout clothes in a special concoction that leaves them smelling like an herb garden, then wrapping them in white tissue paper and returning them to his gym bag. A daily swapping. Something about an exchange of energy. Drawing negativity out of him as he sweats, while drawing in the herbs of the gods. Whatever makes her happy. The things he does that nobody knows about.

Miss Dog stirs, rests her head on his foot. Nana

centers a leaf on a strip of tape. She reaches for a box of matches, lights a Saint Michael the archangel candle in a colorful glass jar, and says, "Someone's poking a stick at something and will pay the price. A very high price."

"Poking a stick at something is her normal routine," he says.

"Not the Husk. Someone else. A nonhuman."

Nana doesn't mean an animal or a rock. Nonhumans are dangerous people incapable of love or remorse. In other words, sociopaths.

"One person comes to mind immediately," Win says.

"No." Nana shakes her head. "But she's in danger."

He reaches across the table, plucks Nana's car keys off the outstretched ceramic arm of a small Egyptian statue, says, "Danger keeps her from getting bored."

"You're not leaving this house, my darling, without putting those bay leaves in your boots."

He pulls off his motorcycle boots, slips in the bay leaves, making sure they're pointing the correct way, according to manufacturer's instructions.

Nana says, "Today is the day of the goddess Diana, and she rules silver and copper. Now, copper is the old metal of the moon. It conducts spiritual energy, just as it does heat and electricity. But beware. It's also used by bad people to channel hoaxes. That's why it's being stolen hand over fist these days. Because falsehoods rule. The dark spirit of hatefulness and lies dominates the planet right now."

"You've been watching too much Lou Dobbs."

"I love that man! Truth is your armor, my darling." She dips into a pocket of her long skirt, pulls out a small leather pouch, places it in Win's hand. "And this is your sword."

He unties the drawstrings. Inside are a shiny new penny and a small crystal.

"Keep them with you at all times," she says. "When put together, they form a crystal wand."

"Great," he says. "Maybe I can turn Lamont into a frog."

Not long after he leaves, Nana carries a box of kosher salt upstairs to her bathroom, where octagonal mirrors hanging in the corners direct negativity back to the sender.

Evil this way bent
Return whence it's sent!

She never goes to bed unclean, lest the unpleasantness of the day continue in her dreams. Unsettledness. She feels the presence of the nonhuman. A childish one filled with mischief and meanness, resentment and pride. She pours salt on the shower floor, turns on the water, and chants another spell.

Rising moon and setting sun,
My sacred work is never done.
Breath and light for me are one.
Warrior of justice, come!

The salt beneath her feet draws bad energy from her and washes it down the drain, and she ends her shower with an herbal brew of parsley, sage, rosemary, and thyme that she boiled in an iron pot this morning. She pours the fragrant water over her head to cleanse her aura, because her work brings her into contact with many personalities, not all of them good, especially this one. The nonhuman. A young one who is ranging about. It is close now and wants something of Nana's, something very dear to her.

"My most powerful instrument of magic is my very being," she says out loud. "I will pinch you between my two fingers!" she warns it.

In her bedroom, she opens a drawer and retrieves a small red-silk bag filled with iron nails, tucks it into the left pocket of her clean, white robe. She sits next to Miss Dog on the bed, writes in her journal by the light of white candles. Writes her usual musings about *Magick* and *Spells* and the *Work of the Mage*. The journal is thick, bound in Italian leather, and she has filled its pages, the pages of many journals for many years, writing in her large, looping script. Then a heavy fatigue, and candles out, and she has one foot into the land of sleep when she sits up with a start in the dark. She grabs the bag of nails out of her robe pocket and jangles them loudly.

Miss Dog, deaf and snoring, doesn't stir.

Footsteps downstairs along the wooden hallway between the kitchen and the living room.

Nana jumps out of bed, jangles the nails again as she flies out the bedroom door.

"I will punish you by the rule of three times three!" she yells.

Footsteps moving fast. *Stomp-stomp-stomp-stomp-stomp.* The kitchen door slams shut. Nana looks out her window, sees a shadow running, carrying something. She hurries down the stairs and out of the house, and wanders about her overgrown property as wind chimes clatter and clang, agitated and angry. She feels the emptiness of what was just there. Then the sound of a car, and far down the street, taillights are the bright red eyes of the devil.

3

Inside the FRONT's mobile crime lab, Stump examines the note from the day's bank robbery, looking for something, anything, foiled again.

Raising latent fingerprints on paper isn't the sure thing depicted on all those cop shows, and in the real world, this bank robber has yet to leave a useful clue. She stops what she's doing as she hears a car pull up. Then her cell phone rings.

"It's me." Win's compelling baritone voice. "You giving tours? I'm outside your big-ass truck."

She pulls off her latex gloves, opens the tailgate. He climbs up the steps, squints in the bright lights as she lets him in, shuts the heavy doors, slam-dunks the used gloves in the trash, yanks a new pair out of a box.

"How did you know I was here?" she asks.

"You had a bank robbery today. Remember?" He moves close to the countertop where she's working. "And let me see. You aren't at your shop. So I called your dispatcher and asked where I might find you."

"You're offensive and presumptuous, and I'm not amused." Pulling on the latex gloves, having a bit of a struggle with them.

"What you got here?"

If there's one thing she detests, it's a guy who's so perfect, he looks like a friggin' Calvin Klein underwear ad and, if that's not annoying enough, assumes he can charm the birds out of the trees. Well, not this tough old bird. Besides, if she runs him off, she's only doing him a favor.

"What I've got is nothing," she says irritably. "It's as if he's wearing gloves, only I know he's not."

"You sure? Absolutely?" He moves closer.

She can smell him. The hint of a spicy, masculine cologne. Probably expensive, like everything else he's got.

"I'm sure this will shock you," Stump says, "but I recognize gloves when I see them." She rewinds the surveillance tape, says, "Help yourself."

The bank's glass front door opening. White guy—or could be Hispanic—acting normal, perfectly at ease, with baggy blue sweats, sunglasses, dark hair, a Red Sox baseball cap pulled low, smart enough to know where the cameras are and to divert his face from them. No other customers inside. Three teller windows, one occupied by a young woman. Smiles as he approaches, slips her the note. She stares at it, doesn't touch it, terror on her face. Fumbles with the cash drawer, fills a deposit bag. He runs out of the bank.

"Another look at his hands." Win leans closer.

She backs up the video, pausing it so he can get a good look at the robber's hands as he's sliding the note under the teller's window. She can feel Win's closeness, as if he heats up the air.

"No gloves," he agrees. "Same thing in the other robberies?"

"So far."

"That's a little strange."

The note from this morning's case is on clean

butcher paper covering the counter, and he stares at it for a long time, as if he's reading an entire page of print, not just the same simple ten words the robber writes on every note.

EMPTY CASH DRAWER IN BAG. NOW! I HAVE A GUN.

She explains, "Neatly written in pencil on a four-by six-inch sheet of white paper, torn from a notepad. Same as the other three cases."

"Watertown, Somerville, now Belmont," Win says. "All of them members of the FRONT, unlike Cambridge, which has yet to join your private club, and . . ."

"And why do you think this is?" she interrupts. "Lamont's headquarters is in Cambridge, and she has her own private club called Harvard, which pretty much owns Cambridge. So could that possibly have something to do with why Cambridge hasn't joined the FRONT and probably never will?"

"I was going to add that your robber also hasn't hit Boston," Win says. "What's going through my mind is Watertown, Somerville, and Belmont border on Cambridge. And Boston is close by as well. Certainly there are a lot of banks in Cambridge, not to mention Boston, yet your robber's avoided both places. Coincidental?"

"Maybe they'll be next." She's got no idea where he's going with this. "If so, I guess yours truly here won't be helping out, since Cambridge and Boston cops do their own crime scene investigation, handle their own evidence."

"That's one point I'm trying to make," he says. "Boston PD has its own labs, and if we're honest about it, Cambridge gets priority with state police labs because of Lamont."

"And because Cambridge hasn't joined the FRONT, and *if we're honest about it,* departments that join us get punished for it. Get treated as if we've committed treason." Rudely. She doesn't know why he seems to bring out the worst in her.

"If I were a smart bank robber," Win continues, "I would definitely pick targets where police resources are limited and the evidence analysis is going to take forever, assuming it's done at all."

"Well, that would be most of Middlesex County. So I'm missing your point."

"My point is maybe you should think about where he's not committing his crimes as opposed to where he is committing them. Let's just say this guy's avoiding Boston and Cambridge. Then why? Maybe for reasons I just cited. Or maybe because he lives in Boston or Cambridge. Is afraid someone might recognize him."

"So maybe you're the one robbing the banks. Since you've got that nice apartment in Cambridge."

"Says who?"

"I check somebody out when he's on my radar screen," Stump says. "You sure live like you rob banks."

"You don't know the first thing about how I live. You just think you do."

She points a latex-sheathed finger at the note, says, "Same spelling and punctuation, same block printing."

"You should wear cotton examination gloves. Latex can smear pencil, some inks. This piece of paper from the same notepad?" he asks.

"Wow. So you know about indented writing, too."

"You used electrostatic detection?"

"Holy smoke. And you know about ESDA, too. You're quite the brain trust. As if we have an ESDA, by the way," she says, annoyed. "And if we'd asked you guys? Well, maybe ten years later you'd get around to it. Anyway, oblique lighting did the trick. Each note shows the impressions of the last note written."

"The guy wants us to know it's him," Win says.

"Us? There's no us. How many times do I have to tell you? And you can quit trying to insert yourself into my life, because it's not going to work. I'm not helping you with your publicity stunt."

"I'm sure Janie Brolin wouldn't appreciate your considering her murder a publicity stunt."

Stump wishes he would go away. For his own damn good.

She says, "Why might this bank robber want us to, quote 'know it's him'?"

"Maybe he's showing off. Maybe he's some kind of thrill seeker—gets off on all this."

"Or maybe he's just plain stupid, doesn't realize each time he writes a note, he leaves indentations of it on the sheet of paper below it," she says.

"What about latent prints? Anything on the other three notes?"

"Nothing. Not one damn fingerprint, not even a partial."

"Okay, then he's not stupid," Win says. "Otherwise, he wouldn't keep getting away with it. Middle of the day. And no fingerprints. Not even partials. You used ninhydrin?"

It is an inexpensive, tried-and-true reagent used to develop latent fingerprints on porous surfaces such as paper. The chemical reacts to the amino acids and other components of oils and sweat secreted from the skin's pores. She tells him it hasn't worked on any of the notes, nor have forensic light sources with various bandwidths and special filters.

"And the tellers aren't touching the notes," Win says.

"Just leave them right where they are. Bottom line? We've got nothing. And unless this dude's wearing magic gloves that are invisible to the naked eye, there's no logical explanation for why he isn't leaving a trace of his identity on what now is four notes. Even in cases where there's no usable ridge detail, people who don't wear gloves leave something. A finger mark. A smear. A partial print from the side of the hand or the palm."

"Surveillance videos in all four cases?" Win asks.

"Different clothing, but looks like the same guy to me."

"You mind if I ask you something?"

"Probably."

"Why did you become a teacher and then quit?"

"I don't know. Why are you wearing a gold watch? You fix some rich person's parking ticket, maybe let him off the hook for driving two hundred miles an hour in his Ferrari or something? Or maybe you really are a bank robber."

"My dad's. Before that, his dad's, before that, Napoléon's—just kidding, although he was fond of Breguets," Win says, holding out his wrist to show her. "According to family legend, stolen. Some of my esteemed relatives in the Old Country could have auditioned for *The Sopranos.*"

"You sure as hell don't look Italian."

"Mother was Italian. Father was black, and a teacher. A poet, taught at Harvard. I'm always curious why people want to be teachers, and it's rare I come across one who felt the calling, went to all the trouble, then quit."

"High school. Lasted two years. The way kids are these days, I decided I'd rather arrest them." Opening cabinets, returning various bottles of chemicals, dusting powders, crime lights, camera equipment, her hands nervous and awkward. "Anyone ever tell you not to stare? It's impolite. You stare worse than a baby," she says, sealing the bank robber's note in an envelope. "Last resort would be to swab for DNA. But no point, in my opinion."

"If he's not leaving sweat, not likely he's leaving DNA, unless he's shedding a lot of skin cells or sneezing on the paper," Win says.

"Yeah. Try wasting state police lab time on that one. Two years now I've been waiting for results on that girl who got raped in the Boneyard. The cemetery near Watertown High School. Not about bones. About smoking joints. Three years I've been waiting for results on the gay guy who got beaten to a pulp on Cottage Street. And forget all the hair salon breaks, what's going down in Revere, Chelsea, on and on. No one's going to take anything seriously until people start getting murdered right and left," she says.

They step out on the truck's diamond-plate steel platform; she shuts the vertical rear doors, locks them. He walks her to her unmarked Taurus, dull paint job, lots of dings on the doors, and she gets inside, waiting for him to stare at her leg, waiting for him to ask some stupid question about how she drives with a fake foot. But he's subdued, seems oblivious, is gazing off at her two-story brick police department, old and tired and much too small. As is true of most departments in Lamont's jurisdiction, no room to work, no money, nothing but frustration.

She starts the car, says, "I'm not going near the Janie Brolin case."

"Do what you gotta do."

"Believe me, I am."

He leans closer to her open window, says, "I'm working it anyway."

Her hand shakes a little as she adjusts the fan, and cool air blows on her face. She says, "Lamont this, Lamont that. And you snap to attention, do whatever she says. Lamont, Lamont, Lamont. No matter what, she gets what she wants and everything turns out great for her."

"I'm surprised you'd say that after what she went through last year," Win says.

"And that's the problem," Stump says. "She'll never forgive you for saving her life, and she'll punish you for the rest of yours. Because you saw her . . . Well, forget it." She doesn't want to think about what he saw that night.

She drives off, watches him in the rearview mirror, wonders where the hell he got that piece-of-junk Buick. Her cell phone rings, and her heart jumps as it occurs to her it might be him.

It's not.

"Done," says Special Agent McClure, with the FBI.

"I guess I'm supposed to celebrate," Stump says.

"Was afraid of that. Looks like you and I need to have another little face-to-face. You're starting to trust him."

"I don't even like him," she says.

*

It's twenty of ten when he parks across the street from the courthouse, surprised to see Lamont's car in her reserved space by the back door.

Just his luck she's decided to work late, and it would be just like her to assume his showing up to clear out some of his desk is a ruse. She's so vain, she'll be convinced his real intention is to see her, that he somehow knew she'd be here at this hour, that he can't stand the thought of not being across the hall from her anymore. What to do. He needs files for court cases, his notes, personal items. It occurs to him it would serve her right if he cleared out his entire office, make her wonder if he's ever coming back. He rolls down his window as his phone vibrates. Nana. Second time she's called in the past hour. This time he answers.

"You're usually asleep by now," he says.

His grandmother keeps odd hours, takes her superstitious shower right after it gets dark. Goes to bed, gets up around two or three in the morning, starts fluttering about the house like a luna moth.

"The nonhuman has stolen the essence of you," she says. "And we must work fast, my darling."

"She's been trying for years, still hasn't touched

my essence." As he watches the back of the courthouse, the top floor lit up. The county jail. Can't get his mind off Lamont. "Don't you worry, Nana. My essence is safe from her."

"I'm talking about your gym bag."

"Don't worry about my laundry, either." He doesn't show his impatience, wouldn't hurt Nana for the world. "I probably won't be able to drop by tomorrow, anyway. Unless you need your car?"

"As I was on the threshold of sleep, the thing came in and I ordered it back out the door. You've gotten mixed up in far more than you bargained for," she says. "It took your gym bag to steal your essence! To wear you like its own skin!"

"Wait a minute." He focuses on the conversation. "Are you telling me someone broke into your house and stole my gym bag?"

"The thing came in and took it. I went out into the yard, then the street, and it drove off before I could pin it inside my magic circle."

"When was this?"

"Soon after it got dark," she says.

"I'm coming over."

"No, my darling. There's nothing you can do. I

cleansed the doorknob, cleansed the kitchen of the evil energy from top to bottom . . ."

"You didn't . . ."

"Eradicated its impure, evil energy! You must protect yourself."

She begins her litany of protective rituals. Kosher salt and equilateral crosses. Draw a pentacle over a photograph of himself. White candles all over the place. Octagonal mirrors on all of his windows. Hold the telephone against his right ear, never the left, because the right ear draws bad energy out, while the left ear draws it in. Finally, she exclaims, "*Something bad's going to happen to the one who did this!*" And her Nana laugh, a good-hearted cackle as he ends the call.

She's always been unusual, but when she gets "on her broom," as he puts it, she unnerves the hell out of him. Her bouts of premonition and clairvoyance, her spates of casting curses and spells, resurrect old feelings of foreboding, distrust, maybe even blame. Magic Nana. What good was she when it came to the worst thing that's ever happened to him? All those promises about what the future held. He could go anywhere, be anything, the world was his to seize. His parents didn't want another child because he was so special, he was enough. Then that night, and Magic Nana never saw it coming and certainly didn't prevent it.

That chilly night when she took her adoring grandson on one of her secret missions, and she had not the slightest sense that something was terribly wrong. How was that possible? Not even the faintest foreshadowing, not even when they got home and opened the door and were greeted by the most absolute silence he's ever experienced in his life. He thought it was a game at first. His parents and his dog in the living room, pretending to be dead.

After that he didn't go on any of Nana's secret missions, has never had any interest in the same mystical guidance so many other people seem to need. All while he was growing up, this parade of strangers in and out of the house. The bereft, the helpless, the desperate, the frightened, the sick. All paying her whatever they could, whatever their commodity might be. Food, hardware, clothing, art, flowers, vegetables, handiwork, haircuts, even medical care. It never has mattered what or how little, but it has to be something. Nana calls it an "equal exchange of energy," her belief that an imperfect ebb and flow of giving and receiving is what causes everything that's wrong in the world.

Without a doubt, it's the root of what's wrong between Win and Lamont. There sure as hell's no quid for her quo. He stares at her retractable-hard-top black Mercedes, as shiny as volcanic glass, about a hundred and twenty grand, forget pre-owned. She doesn't care what she pays, is too proud to ask for discounts, or more likely enjoys the rush of being able to afford sticker price, afford whatever she wants. He imagines what that must be like. To be a lawyer, an attorney general, a governor, a senator, to have money, to have an extraordinary wife and children who are proud of him.

It will never happen.

He couldn't get into law school, business school, a doctoral program—Ivy League or otherwise—not even if he were a Kennedy or a Clinton. Couldn't even get into a decent college, his application to Harvard probably laughed at, didn't matter that his father had been a professor there. Good thing his parents weren't around when his high-school guidance counselor commented that for such a "bright boy," Win had the lowest SAT scores she'd ever seen.

Lamont suddenly emerges from the courthouse back door in a hurry, briefcase, keys in hand, wireless earpiece pulsing blue as she talks on her cell phone. He can't hear what she's saying, but it's obvious she's arguing with someone. She gets into her Mercedes, speeds right past without noticing him, has no reason to recognize Nana's car. He has a funny feeling, decides to follow her. He stays several cars behind her on Broad Street, then on Memorial Drive along the Charles River, back toward Harvard Square. On Brattle Street, she tucks her Mercedes in the driveway of a Victorian mansion worth six, maybe eight, million, he guesses, because of the location and size of the lot. No lights on, looks unlived-in and poorly maintained except that the grass is mowed.

He drives around the block, parks a couple streets away, grabs a small tactical light he always keeps in Nana's glove compartment. He trots back to the house, notices the grass and some of the shrubbery are wet. The irrigation system must have been on earlier. A curtained window dimly lights up, a barely discernible glow, barely wavering. A candle. He moves silently and out of sight, freezes when he hears a back door opening, shutting. Maybe her, maybe someone else. She's not alone. Silence. He waits, contemplates barging into the house to make sure Lamont's all right, has a bad feeling of déjà vu. Last year. Her door ajar, the gas can in the bushes, and then what he discovered upstairs. She would have died. Some people say what happened to her was worse than death.

He continues to wait. The house is dark, and not a sound comes from it. An hour passes. Just when he's about to do something, he hears the back door shut, then footsteps. He ducks behind a tall hedge, watches a dark shape turn into Lamont as she walks alone to her car, carrying something. She opens the passenger door and the interior light goes on. What appears to be sloppily folded linens. She tosses them on the seat. He watches her drive off, no sign of whoever she had been with inside the house. Bizarre thoughts race through his mind. She's involved in something illegal. Drugs. Organized crime. Her recent shopping sprees—maybe she's on the take.

His new assignment—maybe there's more to it than another one of her political charades. Maybe there's a reason she doesn't want him in her office, want him around.

He remains in his hiding place a little longer, then starts exploring the perimeter of the house, his tactical light brightly cutting across damage to the siding where downspouts appear to have been forcefully removed, and along the roofline, more damage, the gutters gone. Copper flashing with a green patina, suggesting the missing downspouts and gutters might have been old oxidizing copper. Through a window by the back door, he can see the burglar-alarm panel. Green light, not armed. He uses the tactical light to tap out a pane of glass, reaches his hand inside, careful not to cut himself, and unlocks the door. He studies the alarm panel. Obsolete, inactive, green light indicates only that power's on. The house smells musty, the kitchen in shambles, appliances ripped out, tarnished copper plumbing parts scattered over the floor.

He walks in the direction of the room he's fairly certain Lamont was in earlier, the beam of light cutting across the dusty hardwood flooring. Footwear impressions everywhere, some of them quite visible, perhaps from people walking through wet grass before entering the house. He crouches, takes a closer look at impressions that have no tread pattern, the familiar teardrop shape left by high-heel shoes. Lamont. Then others. Larger, round-toe, mesh tread pattern, and unmistakable stripe-shaped impression on the heel. Prada or a Prada knockoff. For a confused instant, he wonders if he left them. Not possible. For one thing, he's still wearing his motorcycle boots. He realizes, uncannily, that he forgot his Prada shoes, left them in his gym bag, which now, according to Nana, has been stolen.

There are other shoewear impressions, similar in size but different treads, maybe running shoes, hiking boots, maybe left by multiple people. Or maybe the same two people have been in here multiple times, obviously not always wearing the same shoes. He uses the tactical light for side lighting, takes photographs with his iPhone from three different angles, using a nine-millimeter cartridge from his pistol for a scale. He estimates the size of the Prada or Prada-like shoes is a ten, maybe ten and a half, about his size. He looks around some more, shining the light across ornate light fixtures, crown molding, cornices, and castings, probably original to the house. He finds the room he's looking for, what appears to have been a parlor in the long-ago past.

Footprints everywhere, some of them appearing to be the same as the ones in other areas of the house, and in the middle of the floor is a bare mattress. Nearby is a thick candle, the wax around the wick melted and warm, and an unopened bottle of red wine, a 2002 Wolf Hill pinot noir, same pinot, even the same vintage that Stump gave him earlier today when he talked to her at Pittinelli's. The same pinot, same vintage, of the bottle he accidentally left in his gym bag along with his Prada shoes.

He takes more photographs, returns to the kitchen, and notices something on a countertop that strikes him as peculiar: The torn cardboard and plastic packaging from a disposable camera—a Solo H_2O with a flash. Maybe some insurance investigator taking pictures of the damage to the house. But rather unprofessional to use a disposable camera. He opens cupboards, rummages, finds an old stew pot, two foil pans. Careful how he touches them, he places the bottle of wine in the pot, the candle in one foil pan, and the disposable camera package in the other. One last sweep with his light, and he notices a window that isn't latched, notices disturbed dust on both sides of the glass. More photographs using side lighting, but he doesn't see any ridge detail, just smudges. A lot of peeling paint has been knocked off the sill and the outside of the sash. Could have been done by someone opening the window from the outside and maybe climbing through it.

Stump sounds distracted when she answers her phone. When she realizes it's him, she seems taken aback.

"I thought I made it clear you're on your own," she says authoritatively, as if she might arrest him.

"The 2002 Wolf Hill pinot," he says.

"You're calling me at this hour to tell me what you think of the wine?"

"You said you just got it in. Has anybody bought it? And do any other stores carry it around here?"

"Why?"

Her tone is different, as if she's not alone. An alarm is going off inside him. Be careful what you say.

"Price shopping." He thinks fast. "Uncorked it when I got home. Amazing. Thought I'd get a case of it."

"You're really nervy, you know that?"

"So I was kicking back, started thinking. Maybe you should try it with me," he says. "At my place. I cook a mean veal chop."

"I don't believe in eating baby calves," she says. "And I've got no interest in having dinner with you."

4

Nana's Buick shakes and coughs as the engine turns off, and the driver's door screeches open like a prehistoric bird.

Win pockets the key, wonders why Farouk the landlord is sitting on the back steps, lighting a cigarette. Since when does he smoke, and he's breaking his own rule. No smoking, no lighting matches or grills, not so much as a spark is allowed on the grounds of his nineteenth-century brick apartment building, a former school, impeccably maintained and rented to privileged people. Or in Win's case, to someone who earns his keep. It's past midnight.

"Either you just started a nasty new habit or something's up," says Win.

"An ugly shorty was looking for you," Farouk says, a dish towel under him, probably so he doesn't get dirt on his ill-fitting white suit.

"She calls herself my shorty?" Win says. "Or is that what you're calling her?"

"She say it, not me. I don't know what it is."

"Gang slang for girlfriend," Win says.

"See! I knew she was a gangster! I knew it! That's why I'm this upset! I don't want peoples like that, try very hard to keep things the right way." In his heavy accent. "These peoples you see in your job, they come here, I have to ask you to move out! My tenants will complain and I will lose my leases!"

"Easy going, Farouk . . ."

"No! I let you here for this unbelievable good price to protect me from bad peoples, and then they come here, these very ones you're supposed to keep away!" He jabs his finger at Win. "Good thing no one but me sees her! I'm very upset. Peoples like that show up here, and you let me down. You have to move."

"What did she look like, and tell me exactly what happened." Win sits next to him.

"I come home from dinner and this white girl come from nowhere like a ghost . . ."

"Where? Here in back? Were you sitting out here smoking when she showed up?"

"I got very upset and so I go to visit José across the street to have a beer and see if he know anything about the shorty, ever seen her, and he said no. So he give me a cigarette or two. I only smoke when I get very stressed, you know. I don't want you to have to move, you know."

Win tries again. "What time was it when she showed up, and where were you? Inside your apartment?"

"I just was dropped off from dinner, so I'm thinking maybe nine o'clock, and you know I always come in from back here, and as I walk up these steps, there she is like a ghost out of a movie. Like she was waiting. I never seen her before and have no idea. She say to me, 'Where's the policeman?' I say, 'What policeman?' Then she says, 'Geronimo.' "

"She said that?" Few people know his nickname. Mostly cops.

"I swear," Farouk says.

"Describe her."

"It's hard to see, you know. I should get lights. A cap on, big pants and short. Skinny."

"What makes you think she's involved in gang activity? Aside from my telling you what a shorty is."

"The way she talk. Like a black person even though she white. And very rough talk, street talk, said a lot of bad words." He repeats a few of them. "And when I say I don't know a policeman named Geronimo, because I protect you always, she cuss me some more and say she knows you live here, and she hand me this." He slides an envelope out of his jacket pocket.

"How many times I got to tell you not to touch things if they're suspicious?" Win says. "That's why I had to take your fingerprints a couple years ago. Remember? Because you touched something else some wacko left me?"

"I'm not one of these *sissies* on TV."

Farouk is hopeless with acronyms, thinks CSI is pronounced "sissy." Thinks DNA is *D&A,* refers to drugs and alcohol testing.

"You can get prints, other evidence off paper,"

Win reminds him, knowing it won't do any good. Farouk never remembers, doesn't care.

Certainly this isn't the first time someone has delivered unsolicited communications to the building or has simply shown up uninvited. The downside to Win's living here so long is it's impossible to keep his address a secret. But typically, his unexpected visitors are nonthreatening. A woman he's met somewhere. Now and then, someone who's read about a case, saw something, knows something, and asks around until he or she gets Win's address. More often, some paranoid soul who wants police protection. Sure, people leave him notes, even alleged evidence, but Win's never seen Farouk this upset.

Win takes the envelope, using his fingertips to hold it by two corners, returns to Nana's car, manages to collect his evidence, carry it without dropping anything. Farouk smokes and watches.

"You see her again, you call me right away," Win says to him. "Some nutcase comes looking for me, don't bum cigarettes and sit out here in the dark for hours, waiting for me to show up."

"I don't want those gang peoples. Don't need drugs and shootings around here," Farouk exclaims.

The building is a walk-up, no such thing as elevators back in the Victorian days of reading, writing, and arithmetic. Win carries the pot and pans up three flights of stairs to his apartment—two former classrooms that were connected during the renovation. Added were a kitchen, a bathroom, a window-unit air conditioner. Since he lived here during the construction, helped supervise and keep an eye on the place, he got his way about a number of things, such as preserving the original fir floors, wainscotting, vaulted ceilings, even the chalkboards, which he uses for grocery lists, other reminders of errands he needs to run, and phone numbers and appointments. He sets the evidence on a table, shuts the heavy oak door, locks it, dead bolts it, looks around the way he always does to make sure nothing is amiss, and his mood sinks lower.

After a day of Lamont and Stump, he feels

worse about himself than usual, is depressingly aware of the Oriental rug, the Thomas Moser table, the leather sofa and mismatched chairs, and shelves of remaindered books he got for almost nothing and has such a hard time reading. Everything undesirable or secondhand, from junk shops, yard sales, eBay, Craigslist. Flawed, damaged, unwanted. He slides out his pistol, places it on the dining-room table, takes off his jacket and tie, unbuttons his shirt, sits at his computer, and logs on to a people-search database, enters the address for the Victorian house in Cambridge. He prints out the last thirty-five years of owners and their possible relatives. Other searches reveal the most recent real-estate transaction was this past March when the run-down property was purchased for six-point-nine million dollars by a limited liability company called FOIL. In uppercase. Must be an acronym. He Googles it.

Nothing much. Just a few hits: a San Diego rock band, an educational site called First Outside Inside Last, Freedom of Information Law, Forum of Indian Leftists, a board game that has to do with words and wit.

He can't imagine how any one of them might be connected to a Victorian mansion on Brattle Street, and it crosses his mind to call Lamont and demand an explanation, tell her he knows where she was earlier tonight, that he saw her. Maybe scare her into confessing to whatever she was doing there. He envisions the room with the mattress, the candle, evidence that photographs were taken. He thinks about the vandalism, signs of what appear to be copper theft. And he obsesses over the bottle of wine, the Prada shoe impressions. If someone is setting him up, who and why? And how is it possible Lamont's not involved?

He covers the dining-room table with butcher paper, puts on latex gloves. Pours an ampoule of iodine crystals in a Ziploc bag, places the envelope inside it, seals the bag, and gently shakes it. A minute or two, and he removes the envelope, blows on it, not worried about DNA—the underside of the sealed flap is the best source for that. His warm, moist breath causes a chemical reaction with the iodine. Several fingerprints appear on the paper, turning black as he continues to blow on them. He slits open the envelope, slides out a folded sheet of plain white paper. Neatly printed on it in pink Magic Marker is *Tomorrow morning. Ten o'clock. Filippello Playground. Yours truly, Raggedy Ann.*

Next day, three p.m., London time.

At New Scotland Yard, Detective Superintendent Jeremy Killien gazes out the window at the revolving triangular steel sign in front of the legendary steel building. Usually, the sign's slow spins help him concentrate. But he's nicotine-deprived and irritated. As if he doesn't have enough to do, and then the commissioner drops a bloody bomb on him.

Killien's fifth-floor office, in the heart of the Specialist Crime Directorate, is overwhelmed by the iconography of his life. Books, file folders, the layered civilizations of paperwork that he'll excavate someday, the walls a polite and prestigious crowd of photographs. Margaret Thatcher, Tony Blair, Princess Diana, Helen Mirren—each posing with him in it. He has the expected shadowbox of police caps, patches, and in a corner, a mannequin dressed in a Victorian uniform worn by a bobby whose collar number, 452H, meant his beat was Whitechapel during the era of Sherlock Holmes and Jack the Ripper.

Hell, one lousy cigarette. Is it so much to ask? For the past hour Killien's tried to ignore the urge, and is outraged all over again that after decades of donating his life to the Metropolitan Police Service, he no longer can smoke at his desk or inside the building, has to creep out of the building on the service lift to the enclosed courtyard with its loading bay that stinks of rubbish and get his fix like some homeless person. He opens a drawer, helps himself to another piece of mint-flavored nicotine gum, calms down a bit as his tongue begins to tingle.

Dutifully, he returns to the perusal of this unsolved Massachusetts homicide from 1962. Bizarre. The commissioner must be off his trolley to take on such a thing. An unsolved forty-five-year-old murder that didn't even occur in the UK? Winston "Win" Garano, also goes by the nickname Geronimo. No doubt because of his mixed race. A handsome fellow, Killien will give him that. Mocha skin, wavy black hair, the strong, straight nose of a

Roman emperor. Thirty-four years old, never married, both parents died when he was seven. A faulty heater, carbon monoxide poisoning. Even killed his dog, Pencil. Odd name for a dog.

Let's see, let's see. Raised by his grandmother, Nana . . . Oh, this is a good one. Calls herself a "woman of the craft." A witch. Deplorable driving record. Parking violations, running red lights, illegal U-turns, speeding, license suspended and reinstated by payment of fines. Good Lord, oh, here we go. Arrested three years ago, charges dropped. Seems she flung nine hundred and ninety-nine newly minted pennies on Massachusetts governor Mitt Romney's yard. A better one yet. Wrote Vice President Dick Cheney's name on parchment, placed it inside a bag of "dog poop," buried it in a cemetery. Caught in the act both times, was putting a curse on them. Well, no crime in that. She should have gotten a reward.

It appears Win Garano has been removed from his normal duties, assigned to the Watertown case. Sounds suspicious. Sounds like punishment. Sounds like he's done something to alienate his boss. Monique Lamont, district attorney for

Middlesex County. Despite strong support from the public, she withdrew from the 2006 gubernatorial election, switched to the Republican party, and placed herself back on the ballot for reelection to her current position. Won by a wide margin. Never married, no current significant relationship. Killien stares for a long time at a photograph of her. Dark hair, dark eyes, quite stunning. Prominent family of French descent.

His phone rings.

"Have you had a chance to review the Massachusetts situation?" the commissioner asks him right off.

Situation? That's an unusual way to put it. Killien opens a manila envelope, slides out more photographs, police and autopsy reports. Takes a second for him to realize to his astonishment that the victim is Lamont. Raped and almost murdered last year.

"Hello? Are you there?" The commissioner.

"Looking at it even as we speak, sir," Killien replies, clearing his throat.

The attack took place in the bedroom of her Cambridge, Massachusetts, home, her assailant shot to death by this same detective, Win Garano. What was he doing inside her bedroom? There it is. Concerned by her demeanor on the phone, drove to her house, found the back door ajar, interrupted the assailant and killed him. Crime scene photographs of the would-be murderer on Lamont's bedroom floor, blood everywhere. Photographs of Lamont, of her injuries. Ligature marks around her wrists, her ankles. Suck marks on her fully exposed . . .

"Are you listening to me?" The commissioner's commanding voice.

"Of course, sir." Killien looks out the window at the revolving sign.

"The victim, as I'm sure you're well aware by now, was British. From London," the commissioner says.

Killien hasn't gotten that far, and if he says as much, the commissioner will give him stick about it. Killien avoids answering the question by asking a different one. "This wasn't thoroughly investigated by the Met at the time?" He moves paperwork around on his desk. "I don't see anything . . ."

"We weren't contacted, apparently. There didn't seem to be a British interest, apparently. The victim's boyfriend was American, was the main suspect, and even if there was the slightest suspicion she may have been the work of the Boston Strangler, there wouldn't have been a reason to involve us."

"The Boston Strangler?"

"The district attorney's theory."

Killien spreads out photographs taken at the hospital, where she was examined by a forensic nurse. He imagines the cops seeing Lamont like this. How can they look at their powerful DA ever again and not imagine what's in these pictures? How does she cope?

"Of course I'll do whatever you wish," he says. "But why the sudden urgency?"

"We'll discuss it over a drink," the commissioner says. "I have an event at the Dorchester, so meet me there five sharp."

Meanwhile, in Watertown, Filippello Park is deserted.

Nothing but empty picnic tables beneath shade

trees, vacant playing fields, and cold barbecues. Win figures the *playground* Raggedy Ann referred to in the card she left with Farouk is probably the tot lot, so he waits on a bench near sliding boards and a splash pool. No sign of anybody until eight minutes past ten, when he hears a car on the bike path. There are only two types of people outrageous enough to drive on bike paths: cops or idiots who should be arrested. He gets up as a dark blue Taurus parks, and Stump rolls down her window.

"Understand you're supposed to meet someone." She looks furious, as if she hates him.

"You chase her off?" he says, none too friendly himself.

"You shouldn't be here."

"Believe it's a public park. And what the hell are you doing here?"

"Your meeting's been canceled. Thought I'd drop by to let you know in person. Was considerate about it, even after what you did."

"What I did? And who the hell told you—"

"You show up uninvited at the mobile lab," Stump interrupts. "Spend an hour with me, pretending to be a nice guy, even helpful. Call later and ask me on a date, and all the while you're burning me!"

"Burning you?"

"Shut up and get in. I recognized your car wreck over there. You can get it later. Don't think you have to worry about anybody stealing it."

They creep along the bike path, her dark glasses fixed straight ahead, her dress casual bordering on sloppy, but deliberate. Khaki shirt, untucked, baggy, to hide the pistol on her hip or at the small of her back. Her jeans are loose-fitting, a faded soft denim, frayed in spots, and long, probably to conceal an ankle holster. Most likely her left ankle. Could be on her right ankle, he has no idea. Is ignorant about prosthetics, and he follows the contours of her thighs, wondering what she does to keep the right one as muscular as the left, imagines she must manage leg extensions, maybe on a specially designed machine, or she might wrap weights below the knee and do extensions that way. If it were him, no way he'd let his thigh completely atrophy just because some other part of him was missing.

She suddenly stops the car, yanks up a lever

under her seat to shove it back as far as it will go, and props her right foot up on the dash.

"There," she snaps at him. "Get an eyeful. I'm sick of your not-so-subtle voyeurism."

"Great hiking boots," he says. "LOWAs with Vibram outsoles, shock-absorbing, amazing stabilization. If it wasn't for the brim of the prosthesis socket just above your kneecap—which is visible through your jeans, by the way, only because your leg is bent and halfway in the air—I wouldn't know. I'm not the one having the problem. Curious, yes. Voyeuristic, no."

"You left out manipulative, because that's what you are—a goddamn manipulator who must do nothing but cruise designer-clothing stores, men's catalogs. Because all you care about is the way you look, and no wonder. Since that's all there is to you. And I don't know what you're up to, but this isn't the way to start. First, you were supposed to meet the chief at ten. So already you're demonstrating your lack of respect."

"I left a message."

"Second, I don't appreciate you messing with people who are none of your business."

"What people?"

"The lady you bullied into meeting you at the park."

"I sure as hell didn't bully anyone. She left a note at my apartment building late last night, signed it Raggedy Ann, told me to meet her at the playground this morning." He doesn't realize how ridiculous it sounds until he's said it.

"Stay away from her."

"Thought she was just some crazy from a local shelter. Now suddenly you have a personal relationship."

"I don't give a damn what you thought."

"How did you know I was meeting her?"

Stump shoves the seat forward, starts driving again.

"You know what?" he says. "I don't have to put up with this. Turn around and drop me off at my car."

"Too late for that. You're getting your way. Gonna spend a little time with me today. And maybe by the end of it you'll take my recommendation and go back to your day job and get the hell out of Watertown."

"Oh, before I forget. I was burglarized last night." He's not about to mention Nana, that actually she was burglarized, not him. "Now I find out some fruit loop who dresses like a rag doll is lying about me. Then, magically, you show up instead of her."

"What burglary?" Stump sets aside her hard-ass act for a minute. "You mean your apartment?"

"No. The friggin' Watergate."

"What was stolen?"

"Some personal belongings."

"Such as?"

"Such as I'm not giving you details because right now I don't trust anybody. Including you."

Silence. They turn on Arlington, then Elm, then pull into a remote parking lot of the Watertown Mall, where she backs into a space between two SUVs.

"Car breaks," she says, as if their previous conversation didn't happen. "These jerks tie magnets to strings, drag them along a door to lift up the lock. Or poke a hole in a tennis ball, slam it against the lock so the forced air pushes it open. Of course, the big thing now is these portable navigation systems."

She opens the glove box, digs out a Magellan Maestro 4040 that has a broken adhesive disk. Plugs the charger into the cigarette lighter, wraps the cord around the rearview mirror. The crippled GPS dangles like fuzzy dice.

"People are stupid enough to leave them in their vehicles, in plain view. In my case, I was stupid enough to leave this one in my car, which is used by other cops when I'm off duty. A little different from what you're used to, I imagine? Crown Vics with GPS systems built in, cell phones with unlimited minutes. You know what happens when I reach my limit of minutes? I've got to pay the phone bill myself. And forget a take-home car."

"If I had a take-home car, you think I'd be driving that car wreck, as you so diplomatically described it?"

"Whose is it, anyway? Doesn't go with your designer suits and gold watch."

He doesn't say.

"See that old lady unlocking her minivan?" Stump goes on. "I could throw her to the pavement, be gone with her pocketbook before you could blink. To her, that'd probably be the worst thing that's ever happened in her life. To big shots like you, it's not even reportable."

"Clearly, you don't know me."

"Oh, I know plenty, because I know what you just did." Her dark glasses look at him. "You're worse than I thought. What'd you do? Ride around to local shelters until you found her so you could scare her to death?"

"I told you. She initiated . . ."

"Maybe she did. After you followed her around, terrifying her, taking advantage of her compromised mental state." Stump's antagonism is becoming less convincing.

He's not sure why, but he senses she's putting on a performance and isn't a particularly skilled actor.

"Who is she?" he asks. "And what's with the Raggedy Ann charade?"

"It's who she needs to be. Maybe believes it, maybe she doesn't. Who knows? Doesn't matter."

"It matters. There's a difference between psychotic and eccentric." He watches more shoppers return to their cars, not a GPS thief in sight.

Stump says, "She claims you threatened her. Claims you told her if she didn't meet you in the park this morning, you'd make sure she got locked up every time she stepped out her door."

"She give you some plausible explanation for why I could threaten her?"

"You wanted sex."

"If you believe that, maybe you're the one who's psychotic," he says.

"Why? Because a guy like you could have anyone he wants, so why would he want an unattractive nobody like her?"

"Come on, Stump. If you've checked me out as thoroughly as you say, you know damn well I don't have that kind of reputation."

"Sounds like you don't know what people say about you, don't know the speculations."

"People say all kinds of things about me. But what are you referring to, exactly?"

"What really happened in Lamont's bedroom that night."

He's speechless, can't believe she just said that.

"How do I know the truth?" Stump says.

"Don't push me too far." He says it quietly.

"Just telling you, the speculation's out there. It's everywhere. People—especially cops—who think you were already in Lamont's house when the guy broke in. Specifically, already in her bedroom. Specifically, you could have protected her without killing him, but that might have resulted in people knowing your dirty little secret."

"Take me back to my car."

"I have a right to know if the two of you have ever had . . ."

"You don't have a right to anything," he says.

"If I'm going to have any respect for you . . ."

"Maybe you should start worrying about my having any respect for you," he says.

"I need to know the truth."

"So what if we did? How 'bout that? She's single. I'm single. We're both consenting adults."

"A confession. Thank you." Coldly.

"Why is it so important to you?" he asks.

"It means you're living a lie, you're nothing but a con artist, a phony. That you sleep with the boss, and that leads directly to why she's sent you to Watertown. Must be something in it for you. Especially if you're still sleeping with her. And you probably are. I have no use for people like you."

"No, I think the truth is you're trying really hard

to have no use for me," Win says. "What? It reinforces your view of the universe if I'm garbage?"

"Narcissist that you are, you would think that."

"We didn't," he says. "There. Are you satisfied?"

Silence, as she starts the car, refusing to look at him.

"And I could have, if you really want to know," he adds. "I don't say that to brag. But after the fact, she was . . . how to put this? Very vulnerable."

"What about now?" Stump starts entering an address into her jerry-rigged GPS.

"After what happened to her? She'll always be vulnerable," he says. "Problem is, she'll never know it, just walk into one bad mistake after another. For all her brashness, Lamont runs like hell from herself. For all her smarts, she has no insight."

"That's not what I meant. What about now?"

"Not even close. Where are we going, by the way?"

"I need to show you something," Stump says.

5

The Dorchester Hotel is for heads of state and celebrities, not for the likes of Killien, who can scarcely afford a cup of tea there.

A Ferrari and an Aston Martin are being valet-parked in front as a taxi unceremoniously deposits him in a cluster of kaffiyeh-clad Arabs, who aren't interested in getting out of his way. *Probably related to the Sultan of Brunei who owns the damn place,* Killien thinks as he enters a lobby of marble columns and gold cornices, and enough fresh flowers for several funerals. One advantage to being a detective is he knows how to walk into a place or situation and act as if he belongs.

He buttons his wrinkled suit jacket, takes a left, enters the bar, makes a point of appearing indifferent to the red art glass, the mahogany, the purple and gold silk, the Asians, more Arabs, a few Italians, a couple of Americans. Doesn't seem to be a single Brit except the commissioner, sitting alone at a small, round table in a corner, his back to the wall, facing the door. After all is said and done, at heart the commissioner's still a cop, albeit a well-heeled one because he's made good choices in life, including the baroness he married.

He's drinking whisky, neat, probably Macallan with a sherry finish. Silver dishes of crisps and nuts nearby look untouched. He's impeccable in gray pinstripes, white shirt, dark red silk tie, his mustache neatly trimmed, blue eyes typically vague, as if he's preoccupied, when in fact he doesn't miss a thing. Killien's barely in his chair when a waiter appears. A pint of stout will do. Killien needs to keep his wits about him.

"I need to fill you in about this American case," the commissioner begins, not one for small talk. "I know you're wondering why it's a priority."

"Certainly I am," Killien says. "Haven't a clue

what this is all about, although what I've seen so far is rather curious. For example, Monique Lamont . . ."

"Powerful and controversial. Quite stunning, I might add."

Killien thinks of the photographs. The commissioner would have looked at them as well, and he wonders if his boss shares his same rather unsettling reaction. It's not proper to look at photographs associated with a violent crime and allow one's attention to wander beyond the woman's wounds, into areas that have nothing to do with good policing. And Killien can't stop thinking about the pictures, envisioning her supple . . .

"Are you with me, Jeremy?" the commissioner asks.

"Yes, indeed."

"You seem a bit foggy."

"Not a-tall."

The commissioner says, "So. Several weeks ago, she rang me up, asked if I was aware that a possible victim of the Boston Strangler was a British citizen. Said the case had been reopened, and suggested the Yard get involved."

"Frankly, I don't know why we would do more than make a couple of inquiries behind the scenes. Sounds political to me."

"Of course. She already has extravagant publicity planned, including a BBC special that she guarantees would air if we participate, and so on and so on. Rather presumptuous, as if we need her backing for a BBC endeavor. She's quite bold."

"I don't know how we can help her prove such a theory, since there's no certainty as to the identity of the Boston Strangler. And probably never will be," Killien says.

The commissioner sips his whisky. "Her political agenda is unimportant. I know her type all too well. Ordinarily, her attempt to drag us into such a matter would be politically ignored. But it seems there's an angle she's unaware of, and that's why you and I are having this conversation."

The waiter appears with the pint of stout. Killien takes a big swallow.

"When she first approached the Yard about her very old case, as a courtesy, if nothing else, I had the matter looked into, which included finding out something about her. Just the routine checks," the commissioner continues. "And we've come up with a disturbing bit of information—not about the case, which frankly matters very little to me. But about Monique Lamont herself, and cash transactions and donations that have come to the attention of the US Treasury Department. Turns out her name is in the Defense Intelligence Agency's database."

Killien abruptly sets down his pint of stout. "She's suspected of funneling money to terrorists?"

"Indeed."

"Right off, what comes to mind is some bureaucratic blunder. Perhaps she suddenly made large wire transfers for legitimate reasons," Killien suggests.

Happens more often than people realize. Based on what he read in her dossier, like the commissioner, she's got millions she didn't acquire on her own, likely moves around a lot of money, pays cash for big purchases in America and abroad, makes generous donations to various organizations. Then he remembers something else he just reviewed. Last fall she suddenly changed political parties. In and of itself, that might well have motivated whoever felt betrayed or offended to seek revenge.

"Of most concern, it seems," the commissioner is saying, "is a sizable contribution she recently made to a children's relief fund in Romania. A number of these groups, as you know, are fronts for terrorist fund-raising. The one she gave to, in particular, is suspected of trafficking in orphans, supplying them to Al-Qaeda so they can be used as suicide bombers and such."

He tells Killien there was quite a lot in the press about the donation, about Lamont's compassion for orphans, which leads Killien to suspect that if the relief fund really is a terrorist front, it's doubtful Lamont knows. If she knew, why would she hold a press conference about it? Doesn't matter. You don't have to have intent or awareness to be guilty of a crime.

And the commissioner says, "She's on a no-fly list but is probably unaware of it since she hasn't tried to book a commercial flight in the past several months. When she does, she'll begin to realize she's being watched. Which is why we need to look into this immediately."

"If her assets have been frozen, certainly she would know it."

"CIA, FBI, DIA leave numerous accounts off the freeze list so possible terrorist funding can be monitored. It's likely she has no idea."

This piques Killien's own private fears. You never know who's riffling through your bank account, e-mails, medical records, or favorite sites on the Internet, until one day you discover your assets are frozen or you can't get on a plane, or agents show up at your business or flat and haul you in for questioning, perhaps deport you to a secret prison in a country that denies it uses torture.

"What's all this got to do with the murder of Janie Brolin and our sudden urgency to look into it?" he inquires.

The commissioner motions for the waiter to bring another whisky, says, "It gives us an excuse to look into Monique Lamont."

The State House dome shines over Boston like a gold crown, and as Lamont stares through the dark tinted window of the state police black Expedition, she wonders why twenty-three-karat gilt instead of twenty-four.

A pointless bit of trivia that most assuredly will irk Governor Mather, who touts himself as quite the historian. She's in a mood to throw him off balance as much as possible this morning. To pay him back for snubbing her, and at the same time to remind him of her immense value. Finally, he'll hear her out and realize the brilliance of her crime initiative, the Janie Brolin case, and its immense international implications.

The aide escorting Lamont is chatty. Lamont isn't. She walks with purpose, quite familiar with the hallway, the council chamber, the cabinet room, the waiting room of portraits and handsome antiques, and, finally, the inner sanctum. All that should have been hers.

"Governor?" the aide says from the doorway. "Ms. Lamont is here."

He's behind his desk, signing documents, doesn't look up. She walks in.

She says, "If anyone will know the answer to this, you will, Howard. The State House dome. Why twenty-three-karat instead of twenty-four?"

"I guess you need to ask Paul Revere that." Distracted.

"He covered it in copper," Lamont says.

The governor signs something else, says, "What?"

"In case you're ever asked, I know you wouldn't want to misspeak. Paul Revere covered the dome in copper to make it watertight." She helps herself to a heavy chair upholstered in lavish damask. "The dome wasn't gilded with gold leaf until about a century after that. And I'm fascinated you chose a portrait of William Phips." She studies the severe oil painting hanging over the marble fireplace behind Mather's desk. "Our esteemed governor of Salem witch trial fame," she adds.

One of the perks of being governor is picking the portrait of your favorite Massachusetts governor to hang in your office. It's common knowledge that Mather would have chosen a portrait of himself had it been painted yet. The pious, devil-hating William Phips stares askance at Lamont. She surveys more antiques, the stucco ornaments decorating the walls. Why is it men, especially Republican men, are so crazy about Frederic Remington? The governor has quite a collection of bronzes. *Bronco Buster* on his rampant horse. *Cheyenne* on a galloping horse. *Rattlesnake* about to bite a horse.

"I appreciate your taking the time to see me, Howard."

He muses, "Twenty-three-karat gold gilding the State House dome instead of twenty-four. News to me, but anyway, symbolic, isn't it? Perhaps to remind us that government isn't quite pure."

But the governor is—a pure conservative Republican. White, early sixties, pleasant beatific face that belies the heartless hypocrite behind it. Balding, portly, avuncular enough so as not to appear overbearing or dishonest, unlike Lamont, who is assumed to be ball-breaking and deceitful because she's beautiful, brilliant, enlightened, exquisitely dressed, strong, and quite vocal about her support and even tolerance of those less fortunate than herself. Simply put, she looks and sounds like a Democrat. And would still be one—in fact, would be governor—were it not for her entrusting her welfare to a direct descendant of that witchcraft hysteric Cotton Mather.

"What should I do?" Lamont begins. "You're the strategist. I admit I'm somewhat of a neophyte when it comes to politics."

"I've given this YouTube development some

thought, and you may be surprised by what I have to say." He puts down his pen. "I happen to view it not as a liability but a possibility. You see, Monique, the plain-and-simple truth is, I'm afraid your switching to the Republican party hasn't had the desired effect. The public, more now than before, views you as the quintessential liberal, ambitious woman. The sort who doesn't stay home, raise children . . ."

"It's been quite public that I love children, have a sincere and demonstrable concern about their welfare, especially orphans . . ."

"Orphans in places like Lithuania . . ."

"Romania."

"You should have picked local orphans. Ones right here in America. Maybe a few displaced by Hurricane Katrina, for example."

"Maybe you should have suggested that before I wrote the check, Howard."

"Do you get where I'm going with this?"

"Why you've avoided me since you were elected. I suspect that's where you're going."

"You must recall the talks we had prior to the election."

"I remember every word of them."

"And apparently started ignoring every word of them after all was said and done. Which I consider ungrateful and unwise. So now you've come to me in your moment of need."

"I'll make it up to you, and know exactly how . . ."

"If you're going to be a successful Republican leader," he talks over her, "you must represent conservative family values. Be a proponent of them, a crusader for them. Anti-abortion, anti-gay marriage, anti-global warming, anti-stem cell research . . . Well . . ." Fingertips touching, lightly tapping. "It's not for me to judge, and I don't care what people do in their personal lives."

"Everybody cares what people do in their personal lives."

"I'm certainly not naïve when it comes to emotional trauma. As you know, I served in Vietnam."

This route was not the one she expected, and she begins to bristle.

"After what you went through, it stands to reason you would emerge as someone who has more to prove. Aggressive, angry, driven, perhaps a bit unbalanced. Fearful of intimacy."

"I didn't realize that's what Vietnam did to you, Howard. It saddens me to realize you might be afraid of intimacy. How's Nora, by the way? I still can't get used to thinking of her as the First Lady." Dumpy old housewife with the IQ of a clam.

"I wasn't sexually violated in Vietnam," the governor says matter-of-factly. "But I knew of POWs who were." He stares off to one side, like the painted Governor Phips. "People have compassion about what happened to you, Monique. Only a monster would be insensitive to that terrible event last year."

"Event?" Anger flares. "You call what happened an *event*?"

"But realistically?" He mildly goes on. "People don't give a damn about our problems, our mishaps, our tragedies. We hate weakness. It's human nature. It's animal instinct. We also don't like women who are too much like men. Strength, courage are fine within bounds, as long as they're manifested in a feminine fashion, so to speak. What I'm suggesting is, this YouTube video's a gift. Primping in the mirror. Trying to look alluring in a way men appreciate and women can relate to. Exactly the image you need right now to reverse this strengthening tide of unfortunate speculation that what happened damaged you as a potential leader. Yes, you evoked a lot of public sympathy and admiration at first, but now it's fast moving the other way. You're coming across as distant, too tough, too calculating."

"I had no idea."

"The danger of the Internet is obvious," he continues. "Everyone can be a journalist, an author, a news commentator, a film producer. The advantage is just as obvious. People like us can do the same thing. Turn the table on these self-appointed . . . If I used the word that comes to mind, I'd be as vulgar as Richard Nixon. You might want to consider making your own video and posting it anonymously. Then, after much public speculation, get some loser geek out there to take credit."

Which is exactly what Mather does. She figured that one out a long time ago.

"What sort of video?" she inquires.

"I don't know. Go to church with an attractive widower who has several young children. Perhaps address the congregation with deep emotion, talk about your change of heart—a Road to Damascus conversion experience—that's made you passionately pro-life and a proponent of amending the Constitution to ban gay marriage. Talk about the plight of people and pets displaced by Hurricane Katrina to deflect attention away from your helping orphans who aren't Americans."

"People don't post things like that on YouTube. It has to be a candid moment that's embarrassing, controversial, heroic, something funny. Like that bulldog riding a skateboard . . ."

"Well"—impatiently—"fall down the steps when you're leaving the pulpit. Maybe some usher or, better yet, the pastor, rushes to your rescue and accidentally grabs your breast."

"I don't go to church. Never have. And the scenario is degrading . . ."

"And examining your cleavage in a bathroom isn't?"

"You just said it wasn't. Said it was alluring. Indicated it was compelling and caused people to remember I'm a desirable woman and not some sort of cold-blooded tyrant."

"This is not a good time to be stubborn," he

warns. "You don't have three years before the machinery cranks up again. It's already started."

"Which is why I've asked repeatedly to talk to you about another matter." She seizes the opportunity. "An initiative that you really need to hear about."

She opens her briefcase, pulls out a synopsis of the Janie Brolin case. Hands it to him.

He skims it, shakes his head, says, "I don't care if Win what's-his-name solves it. You're talking front-page news for a day, maybe two, and by election time, no one will care or even remember."

"This isn't about one case. It's about something much bigger. And I must emphasize that this can't be made public yet. It absolutely can't. I'm taking you into my confidence, Howard."

He folds his hands on top of his desk. "Don't know why I would make it public, since it's of no interest to me. I'm more interested in helping you with your self-destruction."

A double entendre if ever there was one.

"That's why I've taken the time to advise you," he says. "To put a stop to it."

What he wants to put a stop to is her. He

despises her, always has, and became her supporter last election only to serve a very simple purpose. The Republicans needed to win every office they possibly could, especially the governorship, and the only way to ensure that was to weaken the Democratic party at the last minute by Lamont's withdrawing from the race. Her doing so for "personal reasons" was a front. Behind it, she and Mather made a deal she now knows he had no intention of keeping. She'll never be a Republican senator or member of congress and, most of all, never serve in his cabinet should he reach his goal of winning the presidency before he's dead. She fell prey to his machinations because, frankly, at the time, she wasn't thinking clearly.

"Now I want you to listen to me," the governor is saying. "This is a foolish, frivolous endeavor, and you don't need more bad publicity. You've already had enough for a lifetime."

"You don't know the facts of the case. When you do, you'll have a different opinion."

"Make your opening statement, then. Change my mind."

"This isn't about a forty-five-year-old unsolved

homicide," she says. "It's about allying ourselves with Great Britain to solve one of the most infamous crimes in history. The Boston Strangler."

The governor scowls. "What the hell's Great Britain got to do with some blind girl getting raped and murdered in Watertown? What has Great Britain got to do with the Boston Strangler, for God's sake?"

"Janie Brolin was a British citizen."

"Who gives a damn unless she was bin Laden's mother!"

"And she very likely was murdered by the Boston Strangler. Scotland Yard is interested. Very, very interested. I've talked to the commissioner. At great length."

"Well, now, that's hard to believe. Why would he even get on the phone with some DA from Massachusetts?"

"Perhaps because he's sincere about what he does, is very secure in who he is," she subtly retaliates. "And keeping in mind it's very much to the advantage of Great Britain and the US to forge a new partnership now that there's a new Prime Minister, and hopefully, soon enough, a new president who isn't . . ." She remembers she's now a Republican, and should watch what she says.

"Partnership in what to do about Iraq, terrorists, yes," Mather retorts. "But the Boston Strangler?"

"I assure you, Scotland Yard is enthusiastic, fully engaged. I wouldn't be pushing ahead if that part hadn't fallen into place."

"I still find it hard to believe . . ."

"Listen, Howard. The investigation's under way. It's already happening. The most extraordinary criminal justice coalition in history. The UK and US fighting together to right a terrible wrong committed against a defenseless blind woman—a nobody in a nothing place called Watertown."

"Well, the whole thing's preposterous." But he's interested.

"If my plan succeeds—and it will—you'll be directly credited, which not only shows you're a crusader for justice and have a heart but pushes you into the international arena. You'll be *Time* magazine's man of the year."

It will be a cold day in hell before she gives him the credit. And if anyone's going to be man of the year, it will be her.

"As intriguing as it might be to think this blind British girl was murdered by the Boston Strangler," the governor says, "I don't see how the hell you're going to prove it."

"It can't be disproved. That's what ensures success."

"You'd better be right about this," he warns. "If it's an embarrassment, I'll make sure it's yours. Not mine."

"That's why we must keep this out of the press right now," Lamont reiterates.

He'll leak it immediately.

"We go public only if it's successful," she says.

He won't wait.

"Which, as I've said, I'm confident it will be," she adds.

Of course, he reads between the lines. She can see his thoughts in his beady eyes. Shallow, cowardly dolt that he is. He'll want the media to be all over this now, because in his limited way of thinking, if her initiative fails, it will be the last straw for her and she probably won't recover. If it succeeds, he'll step forward after the fact and take the credit—which (and this is what he fails to see) will simply serve to make him look like the dishonest, cynical politician he is. The only winner at the end of the day is going to be her, by God.

"You're right," the governor says. "Let's keep it quiet for now, wait until it's a fait accompli."

Revere Beach Parkway, speeding past Richie's Slush with its candy-cane striped roof, heading to Chelsea.

"Not to be confused with the Chelsea in London," Stump says.

"That another fancy literary allusion of yours?" Win says.

"No. Just a beautiful, really hip part of London."

"Never been to London."

The Massachusetts Chelsea, two miles from Boston, is one of the poorest cities in the commonwealth, has one of the state's largest populations of undocumented immigrants, and the highest crime rate. Multilingual, multicultural, crowded and rundown, people don't get along, and their differences often land them in jail or leave them dead. Gangs are a scourge that robs, rapes, and kills simply because it can.

"An example of what happens when people don't understand each other," Stump says. "I read somewhere there are thirty-nine languages spoken around here. People can't communicate, at least a third of them are illiterate. They misinterpret, and next thing you know, someone gets beaten up, stabbed, shot down in the street. You speak Spanish?"

"A few key phrases, such as *no.* Which is Spanish for *no,*" he says.

The landscape continues to deteriorate, one block after another of run-down houses with bars on the windows, lots of check-cashing joints, car washes, as Stump drives deeper into the city's dark, depressing heart while the GPS dangling from the rearview mirror tells her to turn this way and that. They enter an industrial area that in the heyday of the Mob was the ideal drop-off for dead bodies, a squalid, scary square mile of rusting sheds, storage facilities, landfills. Some businesses are legitimate, Stump tells him. Many of them are fronts for drugs, fencing stolen goods, and other shady activities such as "disappearing" cars, trucks, motorcycles, small aircraft.

"Even a yacht once," she adds. "Guy wanted the insurance money, claimed the boat was stolen, trailered it up here and had it crushed into a cube."

His iPhone again. He checks caller ID. Number *Unknown.* Lamont's number comes up that way. He answers, and *Crimson* reporter Cal Tradd's voice is in Win's ear.

"How did you get this number?" Win says to him.

"Monique said I should call you. I need to ask you about the Janie Brolin case."

Goddamn her. She promised nothing was going to be released to the media until the case was solved.

"Look, this is important," Cal goes on. "I need to verify you're on special assignment, and there's a Boston Strangler connection."

"Go screw yourself. How many times I got to tell you I don't talk to reporters . . ."

"Have you been listening to the radio, watching TV? Your boss is furious. Someone leaked all this, and my suspicion is it's the governor's office. I won't name names, but suffice it to say, I know some of the idiots who work down there . . ."

"I'm not verifying anything." Win cuts him off, hangs up on him, says to Stump, "It's all over the news."

She says nothing, is busy driving and swearing at the GPS. It tells her to make a legal U-turn.

6

Stump parks in an alley where they have a good view of DeGatetano & Sons, a scrapyard with mountains of twisted metal behind fencing topped with razor wire.

She says, "You see where we are?"

"I saw where we are before we got here. You must think I spend all my time hanging out in Cambridge coffee shops," Win says.

Tough-looking customers are pulling up in trucks, vans, and cars, all loaded with aluminum, iron, brass, and, of course, copper. Eyes are furtive, guys filling grocery carts, pushing them inside the machine shop, vanishing into a noisy darkness.

"An unmarked Taurus in an alleyway?" she goes on. "We may as well be a Boeing 747. Maybe we should pay attention to our surroundings, because they're sure as hell paying attention to us."

"Then maybe you shouldn't be so conspicuous," he says.

"That's what deterrents do. They're conspicuous."

"Right. Like chasing off cockroaches. Scare them from one corner to the next until they end up at the corner they started from. Why did you bring me here?"

"Chasing off cockroaches is exactly the impression I want people to have—want them to think I'm after petty thieves. Construction workers, installers, contractors, these dirtbags who pilfer metal from construction sites. Some of it scrap, a lot of it not. Bring it here, no IDs, no questions asked, paid in cash, the clients they rip off have no idea. Remind me never to remodel or build a house."

"If you're in and out of here on a regular basis, how come you need the GPS?" he says.

"Okay. So I have a terrible sense of direction.

Don't have one at all." The way she says it, it sounds like the truth. "And I'd appreciate it if you kept that to yourself."

Win notices a thin person in baggy clothes, a baseball cap, climbing out of a pickup truck piled high with copper roofing, pipes, dented downspouts.

"Disorganized crime is what I call it," Stump says. "Unlike the old days when I was growing up in Watertown. Everybody knew each other, would be eating in the same restaurant with the Mafia—same guys who remember your grandmother at Christmas or buy you ice cream. Truth be told? They kept the streets clean of scumbags. Burglars, rapists, pedophiles? They'd end up in the Charles River with the heads and hands cut off."

The thin person he's watching is a woman.

"Organized crime was a good thing," Stump continues. "At least they had a code, didn't believe in beating up old ladies, carjackings, home invasions, molesting little kids, shooting you in the head for your wallet. Or for no reason at all."

The thin woman pushes two empty carts toward her truck.

"Copper. Currently going for about eight grand a ton on the Chinese black market." Stump abruptly changes the subject, looking where Win's looking. "You beginning to understand why I brought you here?"

"Raggedy Ann," he says. "Or whatever her real name is."

She's filling a cart with scrap copper.

"Super Thief," Stump says.

"That whack job?" Win says in disbelief.

"Oh, she's a thief, all right. But not the one I'm after. I want the guy who's doing the major hits. Stripping buildings of plumbing pipes, downspouts, roofing. Ripping off miles of wire from power lines, construction sites, breaking into telephone trucks. Maybe his real deal is drugs—taking the money and buying oxys, then reselling them on the street. These days going for around a dollar a milligram. Drug crimes lead to other crimes, finally lead to violence. Including murder."

"And you think your Super Thief's unloading the stolen copper here," Win assumes.

"Somewhere around here, yes. At this particular fine establishment? Probably one of many he uses."

He watches Raggedy Ann, says, "An informant, I assume."

"Now you're getting it," Stump says.

Raggedy Ann pushes her cart, doesn't seem the least bit uncomfortable, as if she belongs in the dangerous world of Chelsea scrapyards.

"What makes you think it's the same person doing the major hits?" Win asks.

"A detail consistent in most of the big jobs. I believe he's taking pictures. We've recovered the packaging from disposable cameras, always the same brand. A Solo H-two-oh. Waterproof with a flash, go for about sixteen bucks in the store—if you can find them. And on the Internet for six or seven. He leaves them at the scene in plain view."

The mansion on Brattle Street. The vandalism, the missing copper downspouts and gutters, the ripped-up copper plumbing, and the Solo H_2O disposable camera box in the kitchen of a house where Win found evidence he fears was planted, evidence that might lead to him. He almost tells Stump about his stolen gym bag, but doesn't. How the hell does he know who's doing what? He's caught in a web of connections, and the spider at the center is Lamont.

He says, "Any prints on the camera packages you're finding?"

"No luck. The typical reagents didn't work on the paper, and superglue didn't develop any prints on the plastic. But just because you can't see a print doesn't mean it isn't there. Maybe the labs will have some luck, because they certainly have more space-age instruments than I do. If they ever get around to it."

He almost asks if she's ever heard of an LLC called FOIL, but he doesn't dare. Lamont spent more than an hour inside that abandoned Victorian mansion. Who was she with? What was she doing?

"Let me ask you something, for the sake of speculation," he says. "Why would your copper thief take photographs at his crime scenes?"

"The first thing that comes to mind," she replies. "He gets off on it."

"Sort of like your bank robber who maybe gets off on leaving the same type of note every single time? Gets off on flaunting himself, letting everybody know he's the same guy doing all of them and not leaving a fingerprint or even a partial, even though you can see in the surveillance tapes that he's not wearing gloves?"

"Are you suggesting it might be the same guy doing all of this? The bank robberies and the copper thefts?" she asks skeptically.

"Don't know. But perpetrators who flaunt their crimes and taunt the police aren't your average bear. So to have two crime sprees in the same geographic area at the same time, and both have what appear to be the MO I'm describing, is extremely unusual."

"Didn't realize you're a profiler, in addition to all of your other talents."

"Just trying to help."

"I don't need your help."

"Then why am I sitting here? You could have told me this Raggedy Ann weirdo is an informant so I'd understand why I should stay away from her. You didn't need to show me."

"Seeing is believing."

"You going to tell me her name, or am I supposed to call her Raggedy Ann for the rest of my life?"

"You won't know her for the rest of your life. I

can promise you that. I'm not telling you her name, and here are the rules." Stump looks across the street. "You've never seen her before, and she's never seen us and has no interest. We're down here because I just happened to drop by. No big deal. As I've explained, I do it from time to time."

"I assume you're going to act as if you don't know her, either."

"You assume right."

Raggedy Ann pushes the cart inside the shop.

"The guy who runs this yard is Bimbo—biggest juicehead in Chelsea. Thinks he and I are pals. Come on," Stump says.

Eyes are on them from every direction as they get out of the car and cross the street. The shop is filthy and loud, men cleaning and separating metal, cutting it up, stripping it of nuts, bolts, screws, nails, insulation. Tossing it in piles, clinking and clanking. Raggedy Ann parks her cartful of copper on a floor scale, same kind used in morgues to weigh bodies, and a man emerges from a pigsty of an office. He's short, with heavily gelled black hair and a steroid body, bulky as a bale of hay.

He says something to Raggedy Ann and she drifts back out of the shop. He motions to Stump, says, "So, how's it doing?"

"Want you to meet a friend of mine," she says.

"Yeah? Well, I've seen him somewhere before. Maybe in the paper," Bimbo says.

"That's because he's state police, and he's been in the paper, on TV, because he had to kill a guy last year."

"I sort of remember that. The guy who did the DA."

"He's okay or he wouldn't be here," Stump says of Win.

Bimbo is staring at him, then decides, "You say he's okay, I believe you."

"Seems like he had a little problem in Lincoln. Two nights ago. Another hit, and you know what I'm saying," Stump says.

"A lot of stuff coming in," Bimbo says. "What got hit?"

"Huge house, four million dollars. Right before they were going to hang the drywall, someone comes in and rips out all the wiring. Now the builder's got to hire round-the-clock security so it doesn't happen again."

"What do you want?" Bimbo shrugs his huge shoulders. "Copper don't talk to me. I got in a lot of wire the last two days, already at the smelter."

Raggedy Ann pushes in another cart loaded with scrap copper, parks it on the scale. She pays no attention to Stump, to Win. They don't exist.

Bimbo says to Stump, "I'll keep my eye out. Last thing I want is that kind of thing going on. I run a clean business."

"Right. A clean business," Stump says, as she and Win walk off. "The only thing not stolen around here is the damn pavement."

"You just gave me up to that dirtbag," Win says angrily, as they climb back into her car.

"Nobody down here cares who you are. As long as Bimbo doesn't. And now he's cool with you, thanks to me."

"Thanks nothing. You don't get to give me up to anybody without my permission."

"You're now on the FRONT's turf. You're a guest, and the house rules are ours, not yours."

"Your turf? Am I hearing a different song? Seems like as recently as this morning you didn't want me on your turf. In fact, you've told me more than once to get lost."

"My introducing you to Bimbo's part of the game. It tells him you're with me, so if he sees you again—or anybody else does, no big deal."

"Why would he ever see me again?"

"Always a good chance somebody will get murdered down here. So it's your jurisdiction. I just got you a passport. You don't have to thank me. And just in case you didn't understand what I meant about Raggedy Ann? Now you know I'm serious. Avoid her."

"Then tell her to quit writing me notes."

"I have."

"You said she's a thief. That's how she got the copper?"

"The copper you just watched her unload wasn't stolen. I've got a contractor friend who does me a favor. I give her enough scrap to get her to Bimbo's once, twice a week."

"Does he know she's an informant?"

"That would kind of defeat the purpose."

"I'm asking if he or anyone suspects it."

"No reason to. She's into everything, has been for years. A shame. Came from a really good family but like a lot of kids, got into drugs. Heroin, oxys. Eventually started tricking, stealing, to support her habit. Did two years in prison for stabbing some guy who was pimping her—mistake was not killing the SOB. She gets out of prison and was right back at it. I got her into a meth clinic, into protected housing. Long and short of it, she's valuable to me and I don't want her dead."

As they drive past more rusting sheds, bump over railroad tracks, her cell phone rings several times. She doesn't answer it.

"I lost one a couple of Christmases ago," she goes on. "Got burned by a task force cop who had sex with her, decided to name her in an affidavit so no one would believe her if she ratted him out. So he rats her out first. Next thing, she's got a bullet in her head."

Her cell phone rings again, and she pushes a button to silence it. Four times now since they left the scrapyard, and she doesn't even look at the display to see who it is.

The state police forensic labs have a simple but basic protocol: Evidence you submit should be incontrovertibly associated with crime.

What Win has in several brown paper bags isn't incontrovertibly associated with anything except his own fears, his own sense of urgency. If Lamont is involved in something sinister and is implicating him, he intends to find out privately before he does anything about it. Imaginative guy that he is, it's the *why* part of the equation that has him completely bewildered and unnerved. Why would someone break into Nana's house and apparently steal nothing but his gym bag? Why would this person even know about Nana in the first place, or that Win stops by her house almost daily to check on her, or that he routinely leaves his gym bag because of her laundry magic, or that she routinely fails to lock her doors or set her alarm, making it simple to enter, grab, and run?

Inside the lab building, an officer named Johnny mans the front desk, engrossed in whatever he's looking at on his computer screen.

"How ya doing?" Win says.

"You seen this?" Pointing at the screen. "Friggin' unbelievable."

He plays the YouTube clip of Lamont in the

ladies' room. It's the first Win's heard of it, and he analyzes it carefully. Green Escada suit, Gucci ostrich-skin pocketbook, and matching high-heel shoes, obviously filmed at the John F. Kennedy School of Government. He recalls that minutes after her lecture, she sent him away to get her a latte, and for about an hour, she was out of his sight. Irrelevant, he reasons. It wouldn't have been a big deal for someone to hide in the ladies' room as long as the person had thought this whole thing out, and obviously, someone put a lot of thought into it. Preplanning. A recon to see when she was going into the ladies' room, making sure it was empty before hiding in a stall. A woman. Or some-one dressed like one. Could have been a man, if no one was looking.

"Was a lousy thing to do," Johnny is saying. "Someone did that to my wife, I'd kill 'em. Looks like you got a mess on your hands, though. Mick was in the director's office not even an hour ago, about the . . . What's her name? The murdered lady from the blind school that's all over the news."

"Janie Brolin."

'That's the one."

"Lamont probably sent Mick down here because she's worried about any alleged evidence, although I can't imagine anything relating to the case still exists. Regardless, she'd want to make sure none of the scientists talk to reporters," Win says. "That's what I think, anyway."

"So don't I." A Massachusetts native's weird way of saying *So do I.* "To give her credit? Wow." Shakes his shaved head, watching Lamont on YouTube again. "She's so cold, you forget she's hot, you know what I'm saying? She's got some set of . . ."

"Tracy around?" Win says.

"Let me buzz her." Can't take his eyes off Lamont in the ladies' room.

Tracy's in, and Win follows a long corridor, bypasses evidence intake, walks into Crime Scene Services, where she's seated at her computer station, looking at two enlarged fingerprints on a split screen, arrows pointing to minutiae she's visually comparing.

"We're having a little argument," she says, not looking up.

Win sets down his paper bags.

She points to the left side of the screen, then to

the right. "Computer counts three ridges between these two points. I'm counting four. As usual, the computer isn't seeing what I'm seeing. My fault, was in a hurry, didn't clean it up first, took a short-cut and ran it through auto Encode. Anyway, what can I do for you? Because whenever you drop by with little brown paper bags, it's a clue."

"A sort of official case, and another case that isn't official at all. So I'm really just asking for a favor."

"Who, you?"

"Can't tell you the details."

"Don't want to know. Ruins my objectivity and reinforces my basic belief that everybody's guilty."

"Okay. One Fresca can I fished out of the trash the other day. One Raggedy Ann note and envelope, don't laugh. Prints on the envelope. Could be from my damn landlord, whose prints you have in the database for exclusionary reasons, since he's touched stuff in the past. I didn't mess with the note, and the sender isn't really in doubt, but I'd like these items checked, including DNA under the envelope's flap and on the Fresca can, if you can beg, borrow, and steal from your DNA pals. We've also got a candle and a bottle of wine, a very nice pinot, may have my prints on it. Maybe the lady in the wineshop, whose prints will also be in the database for exclusionary reasons, since she's also a cop. I've got photographs of shoe impressions, and the nine-mil cartridge I used for a scale. Didn't have a ruler handy, sorry."

"And what is it you want me to do with these shoe impressions?"

"Hang on to them for now, in case we recover something to compare them with." Such as his pair of stolen Prada shoes, should they ever surface.

"Finally," he says, "there's the packaging from a disposable camera."

"We've gotten in a number of them of late from different departments, all Middlesex County."

"I know, and the cops think you can't be bothered."

"I really can't be bothered," she says. "Their crime scene guys haven't found anything on them, and send them in anyway, in hopes we have a magic wand, I guess. Maybe they watch too much TV."

"You talking about the FRONT's crime scene guys?"

"Probably," she says.

"Well, that would be one guy, who's a woman, and she doesn't believe in magic wands," Win says. "And since my disposable camera package is the same kind as the ones you've already gotten, how about we make them a priority, a *do-it-now* sort of thing. And I have an idea."

"Whenever you come in here with your trick-or-treat bags, it's a *do-it-now* sort of thing, and you always have ideas."

"What would you expect a copper thief to have all over his person, including his hands?" Win asks.

"Dirt. Since he's probably touching dirty old oxidized gutters, roofing materials, all kinds of crap at construction sites . . ."

"Forget dirt. I'm talking about what might not be visible," Win says. "I'm talking microscopic."

"You want to examine these damn camera boxes under a microscope?"

"No," he says. "Luminol. I want you to check as if you're looking for blood."

He's ordering an iced coffee at Starbucks when he feels somebody behind him. Glances around. Cal

Tradd.

At least he has the decency not to strike up a conversation in a public place. Win pays, grabs napkins, a straw, heads outside and waits by his car, waits for an overdue confrontation. In a few minutes, Cal appears, sipping one of those coffee drinks that looks like an ice-cream sundae. Piled high with whipped cream, chocolate, a cherry on top.

"You following me?" Win asks. "Because I'm feeling followed."

"I'm that obvious, huh?" Licking whipped cream, wearing nice sunglasses. Maui Jim's, about three hundred bucks. "Actually, I was heading to the police department. Probably just like you are. Otherwise, I don't think you'd be jarring your already jangled nerves with several shots of espresso at a Starbucks in little ole Watertown. Anyway, noticed your car."

"Really? How'd you know it was mine?"

"I know your apartment building. Matter of fact, almost rented a place there my freshman year. Second floor, the south end, overlooking that teeny-tiny square of blacktop in back where Farouk lets you park your Ducati, your Harley, your Hummer, this thing"—indicating the Buick—

"whatever you happen to be riding or driving."

Win stares at him, sunglasses to sunglasses.

"Ask Farouk. He'll remember me," Cal says. "Skinny little blond kid whose overly protective mother decided her precious, fragile boy couldn't possibly live in your former school building. Not that the location's dangerous, in reality. But you know how people make judgments based on a person's appearance, demeanor, socioeconomic status. And here I am—rich, a musician, a writer, straight A's, faggy-looking. A walking hate crime waiting to happen." Dips his tongue back into the whipped cream. "I saw you that ill-fated day, by the way. No reason you'd remember. But we were leaving and you trotted by, jumped in your unmarked Crown Vic and sped off. And my mom said, 'Good God in heaven, who's that gorgeous man?' Small world, huh?"

"Save your six-degrees-of-separation crap for someone else. I'm not talking to you," Win says.

"I didn't ask you to talk. You'd be better off listening." Watching traffic go by on Mt. Auburn Street, a major thoroughfare that connects Watertown to Cambridge.

Win opens his car door.

Cal sucks on the straw, says, "I've been working on an investigative series about copper thefts—an international problem, huge, as you well know. There's this nutcase woman. Cunning in some ways, stupid in others, and overall, crazy."

Raggedy Ann, Win thinks.

"I've seen her around in places and situations that have my antenna up—way up," Cal continues. "There's this guy Bimbo. A real Ali Baba scumbag. I've interviewed him a couple times. So maybe three hours ago, I show up at his den of thieves to talk some more, and there she is, collecting cash from him. Same weirdo I've seen around Harvard Square, dressed all freaky like Raggedy Ann. Same weirdo I've seen hanging around Monique on a number of occasions."

"Hanging around her? How so?" Win leans against the car, crosses his arms.

Cal shrugs, sips his chocolaty coffee. "Places where she's given talks, doing press conferences, outside the law school, the courthouse. I've seen this weirdo lady at least half a dozen times in the past few weeks, always dressed in tights, clunky shoes. I didn't think much about it until I recognized her at the scrapyard today. Dressed completely differently, in baggy clothes, a baseball cap. Selling scrap copper. I just thought you'd want to know."

"You ask what's-his-name about her?"

"Bimbo? Sure did. Said the expected. Didn't know anything. Translated, she's selling stolen stuff, right?"

"Then what?"

"Followed her for a while. She has this Woodstock-era VW van, curtains in the windows, probably sleeps in the damn thing. We're not even across the Mystic River when I get this feeling somebody's following me. Another van. This one a construction-type van, maybe one I'd seen earlier at Bimbo's. So I got the hell out of Dodge, got off in Charlestown."

"You mean the intrepid reporter gave up the chase?"

"These copper thugs in Chelsea, you kidding me?" Cal says. "Screw with them and you end up in a car trunk with your throat cut."

7

A sergeant lets Win into a cramped, dank space, dimly lit, nothing inside but old metal filing cabinets and shelves stacked with dusty logbooks and boxes. The Watertown Police Department's records room is a former bank vault, one floor below the jail.

"I don't guess you have some sort of reference system for what's in here," Win says.

"Oh, I'm sorry. The librarian's out sick today and her ten assistants are on vacation. You find what you want, pull the record. No photocopying. No pictures. You can take notes. That's it."

The air is thick with dust and the smell of mold. Already Win feels his sinuses closing up.

"How about I find what I need and you put me upstairs someplace. Maybe in the detective division," Win says. "An interview room would work."

"Jeez, more bad news. The UN's in town, tying up the conference room. The records got to stay in here, meaning if you want to look at them, you got to stay in here."

"This the only light?"

Fluorescent light tubes, one dead, the other losing its will to live.

"Can you believe it? All our maintenance guys are on strike." The sergeant disappears with his big ring of keys.

Win turns on his tactical light, swipes it over shelves of large logbooks, decades of them going back to the twenties. No way. Without photocopies, he'll never get through these reports, would be like bushwhacking his way through a jungle without a machete. Under ordinary circumstances, given plenty of time, he manages to sort through dense pages of information, or, best of all, he's *so busy* he has one of the clerks in the unit read aloud on CD, which he downloads into his computer as an audio file. Amazing what he listens to as he drives, works out in the gym, jogs. By the time he goes to court, he's memorized every pertinent detail.

He climbs a stepladder, pulls down the log for 1962, looks for a work space, resorts to an open file drawer, places the log on top of it, starts flipping through pages, starts sneezing, his eyes itching, miserable. April 4, and he finds the handwritten entry for Janie Brolin's murder. He jots down the location of the crime—meaning her address, since she was murdered inside her apartment—and that one simple fact completely changes the scenario. He can't understand it. Nobody noticed? The Boston Strangler? You've got to be kidding. He keeps going through drawers. Cases aren't filed alphabetically but by an accession number that ends with the year. Her case is WT218-62. He scans labels on file drawers, opens what should be the right one, finds records jammed together so tightly he has to take out sections of them at a time or he can't see what's there.

He pulls the Brolin case, then riffles through

dozens of files in the same drawer, having learned long ago it's not uncommon for information from one file to accidentally find its way into another. After an hour of itching, sneezing, his mouth tasting like dust, he comes across an envelope wedged in the back of the drawer, and written on it is the Brolin case number. Inside is a yellowed newspaper clipping about a twenty-six-year-old man named Lonnie Parris, struck by a car while crossing the street near the Chicken Delight on Massachusetts Avenue in Cambridge. A hit-and-run that occurred in the early-morning hours of April 5—the day after Janie Brolin's murder. That's it. Just an old newspaper clipping.

Why the hell would a hit-and-run have the Brolin case number on it? He can't find the file for the Lonnie Parris death, probably because it's a Cambridge case. Frustrated, he tries his iPhone, can't get on the Internet or even make a call from down here in this cave. He leaves the records room, trots up a flight of stairs, finds himself in the jail's booking room. Cameras, a Breathalyzer, property lockers, and handcuffs dangling from nails along the walls to make sure prisoners behave while waiting their turn to be fingerprinted and have their mug shots taken.

Dammit, no signal in here, either. He steps behind the desk to try the landline phone but doesn't know the code to dial out.

"Stump? That you?" A loud voice startles him.

The jail cells, some inmate. Female. Probably held until she can be transferred to the jail on the top floor of the Middlesex County courthouse.

"I've had enough now, okay, already?" The voice again. "That you?"

Win walks past empty cells, heavy metal doors open wide, catches the faint ammonia stench of urine. The fourth cell door is shut, and posted on it is Q5+. The code for suicide risk.

"Stump?"

"I can get her for you," Win says, peering through the small mesh window, not believing what he sees.

Raggedy Ann sits cross-legged on a slab of a bed inside a cinder-block cell not much bigger than a closet.

"How you doing?" he says. "You need something?"

"Where's Stump? I want Stump!"

On the wall next to the door is a collect telephone for prisoners. It has a direct line out, and across from it on a windowsill is a bottle of hand sanitizer.

"I'm hungry!" she says.

"What they got you locked up for?"

"Geronimo," she says. "I know you."

Now he's hearing her accent, remembers what Farouk said about the so-called shorty. A white woman who talked "black."

"You know me? How's that? Except for our running into each other now and then," he says, nicely enough.

"I don't got nothing to say to you. Get out of my face."

"I can get you something to eat, if you want," he says.

"Cheeseburger, fries, and Diet Coke," she says.

"Dessert?" Win asks her.

"I don't eat nothing sweet."

Fresca, Diet Coke, nothing sweet. Kind of unusual for a junkie, he thinks. Most recovering heroin addicts can't get enough sugar. At least one good thing about looking through a metal mesh-covered window, he can study her without being obvious. Same baggy clothes she had on at the scrapyard. Her sneakers still have their laces. Unusual for a suicide risk. Of course, the jail cell has no towel racks, no window with bars, not even handles on the stainless-steel sink. Nothing to loop a belt, shoelaces, or even clothing around if you wanted to hang yourself.

Without her freakish rag doll getup, she looks more like a street urchin who might be pretty were it not for her curly red hair sticking up everywhere, her nervous mannerisms. Plucking at her fingers. Wetting her lips. Rapidly tapping one of her feet. No matter what he's heard about her, he can't help feeling pity. He knows that people don't grow up fantasizing about being a drug-addicted prostitute or a homeless person who eats out of garbage cans. Most tormented souls who end up like Raggedy Ann started out with bad genetic loading, or abuse, or both, and their subsequent debilitating problems are hell on earth.

He picks up the receiver of the red wall phone, wipes it down with the hand sanitizer, and places a collect call.

*

The operator tells Stump that Win Garano is on the line and will she accept charges.

"You're calling me collect?" she says. "Where are you?"

"Your jail." His voice. "I don't mean in it."

She tenses up. "What happened?"

"Dropped by your records room. My cell phone wouldn't work in there. Looked for a landline and guess who's staying at your charming little B and B?"

"What's she told you?"

"She needs to see you. Wants a cheeseburger. Excuse me." Obviously to Raggedy Ann. "How you want that cooked?" A murmur. Then back to Stump. "Medium, hold the mayo. Extra pickles."

"I'm rather busy at the moment. I realize you've probably forgotten I moonlight as a successful businesswoman." Stump holds the phone between her shoulder and ear, places a block of Swiss on the slicer.

It's that time of day when customers come in all at once, and there's a long line at the deli counter. One impatient woman is waiting to be rung up, and two more people are walking in. Pretty soon—

thanks to Win—she's going to lose control over every aspect of her life. *Damn him.* Wandering into the jail. If that isn't her bad luck. All he seems to bring her is bad luck.

"She's also getting cranky," Win adds.

"I'll be right there," Stump says to him. To the pushy woman at the deli counter, she says, "Be with you in just a minute."

"What's a good wine with smoked salmon?"

"A dry Sancerre or Moscato d'Asti. Third aisle." Back to Win. "Just tell her I'm on my way, and then get out of there and wait for me. I'll explain."

"You want to give me a hint?"

"Safekeeping. Had a little problem after I dropped you off at your car."

Never occurring to her, of course, that he intended to end up at her department, in the records room. Even if she'd known, she wouldn't have assumed he might take a tour of the damn jail.

"Wait a minute. She's saying something to me. Oh, yeah. Add fries, and I forgot the Diet Coke." His voice.

The feeling it gives her. The feeling he gives her, and it's getting worse. She doesn't know what she's going to do. It wasn't supposed to be like this. It was supposed to be relatively simple. He would show up at the department, work Lamont's case, and leave. Even the chief said this trumped-up investigation wasn't Stump's problem and not to worry about it or get involved. *Jesus God.* In the beginning, this was all about Lamont. Win was a minor character and now has gotten bigger than the great outdoors.

"Meet me in the parking lot in twenty, thirty minutes," Stump says to him.

He's inside Nana's car, waiting, when a red BMW 2002 pulls up next to him.

"I'm impressed," he says, as Stump rolls down her window. "Nineteen seventy-three, looks like the original paint job and bumpers. Verona red? Always wanted one of these. Black leather looks original, too. Only the seals and window felt look new. From here, I mean. You had this since you were what? Five, maybe six?" He notes the Wendy's bag in the backseat, adds, "So what happened to land your special friend in jail for safekeeping?"

"Soon as she left Bimbo's, she went to Filene's."

"How does she get around? Been meaning to ask."

"Piece-of-junk Mini Cooper. She ended up at Filene's, shoplifted some makeup and a Sony Walkman."

"That makes her a suicide risk?"

"Q-five-positive status signals the department to check on her, but she's unstable, easily set off. In other words, just the sort you prefer to avoid."

"Anybody ever mention you're a lousy liar?" Win says. "Filene's doesn't carry electronics. Not possible she shoplifted a Walkman. And I don't think she drives a Mini Cooper."

"Why can't you pick up signals? Quit interrogating me about things that are none of your concern."

"I pick up on signals just fine. Especially when they're as subtle as a sonic boom. Here's a hint. Don't fabricate details about places you've never been, like big discount department stores that don't have private, spacious dressing rooms and a small, discreet staff. Not that I'm assuming you take off your prosthesis when you try on jeans, slacks, for example. But if nothing else, you probably have a few select places you frequent—probably small places, boutiques, maybe, where they know you."

"There was a problem after we left the scrapyards," Stump says. "She attracted attention from the wrong person, someone who followed her."

"Got any ideas?" To see if maybe, just maybe, Stump might tell the truth.

"Said some van, like a construction van. She was scared maybe some bad dude from the scrapyards got suspicious, followed her. She freaked out, called me, and I had her pulled by a marked car and arrested."

"Charged with what?"

"Said I had a warrant for her arrest, and she called to turn herself in. Said she'd been charged with selling stolen copper."

"You said it wasn't really stolen. Was like flash money. And you can't arrest somebody without a hard copy of a warrant . . ."

"Look. The point was to ensure her safety. End of story. I had her locked up. If she really was being followed, then whoever was doing it had ample opportunity to see her pulled, cuffed, put in the back of the patrol car. I'll let her out once it's dark."

"This mean she's done at the scrapyards?"

"If she doesn't go back at some point, it will confirm the suspicion there might be something up with her. That maybe she's working with the police. Assuming it's true that someone from the scrapyards was following her."

He passes on what Cal told him.

"Great. All I need is a damn reporter screwing with things," she replies. "These people are ruthless. He'd better watch out he doesn't get himself killed. What are you doing down here?"

She looks good in her red BMW, and her face is pretty in the late-afternoon light.

He says, "My, how quickly we forget. My mundane assignment of solving a forty-five-year-old homicide that might be connected to the Boston Strangler. Even though I know it can't be."

"Amazing if you've already determined that. In fact, I'd call it miraculous. You divine it, or what?"

"A glance at your records. You know much about the history of the Mafia in this quaint town of yours?"

"As I've mentioned before, my quaint town was a better place in the heyday of the Mob. Don't quote me."

"The apartment complex she lived in was on Galen Street, about a two-minute walk from Piccolo's Pharmacy, which isn't there anymore, of course."

"And?"

"Southside. Huge Mob neighborhood. Most of the apartments and houses all around Janie Brolin were occupied by Mob guys. All kinds of stuff going on, whatever you wanted. Numbers, jewelry, prostitution, illegal abortions, all around Piccolo's Pharmacy, Galen and Watertown streets. Why do you think there was no crime down there in the days of yore? I mean none."

"Where the hell do you get all this?" She cuts the engine of her BMW. "You see some movie or something?"

"Just things I've heard over the years, a few books here and there. You know, I'm in the car a lot. Listen to them on tape, CD, have an okay memory. Janie Brolin was murdered on April fourth. A Wednesday. Wednesdays were collection day, all kinds of people showing up to get paid by the bookies. Always the same day, eyes and ears all over the place. So you should think about that. Why was she an exception to the rule, the only murder—ever—in Southside during the early sixties, especially on collection day. Plus the Feds doing their thing. So ask yourself. The cops, the Feds didn't know who killed the girl? You really believe that?"

Stump gets out of her car, says, "You'd better not be making this up."

"Gives me the feeling the cops were in on it. As in a cover-up. You know the old saying, Don't screw with a Mafia guy unless you've got one with you."

"Translated?"

"Collusion. A team effort. Not a sexual homicide at all, period. You remember who was president in 1962?" he says.

They start walking toward the police department.

"Damn," she says. "Now you're really spooking me."

"Right. JFK. Before that he was a senator in Massachusetts, born right over there in Brookline. You know the theories about his assassination. The Mob. Who knows? Probably never will. But my point is, some Boston Strangler lowlife wouldn't have dared step foot anywhere near Janie Brolin's apartment. And if he was so stupid he didn't know any better, he would have ended up in the Dorchester Bay, dismembered, an ax buried in his chest."

"You've got my attention," Stump says.

An hour later, both of them are in the records room, going through Janie Brolin's case file. She's using his tactical light, and he's taking notes.

"Your clout and we can't go to your office or something?" Win says, his eyes and throat itching again.

"You don't understand. There are four of us in one small office, not including the house mouse." Meaning the administrative officer. "Everybody hearing everything the other person's saying. Cops talk. Do I need to tell you that?"

"Okay. The weather." Win flips back through his notes. "Anything about the weather on April fourth?"

"Not on any of these reports." Stump has Janie Brolin's file open, doing what Win did earlier, using a drawer as a table because there's nowhere else to work.

"What about newspaper articles?" he asks.

She looks at a few. Old, sharp creases from having been folded for more than forty years.

She says, "A mention that when the police arrived at her apartment around eight a.m., it was raining."

"Let's go over what we know so far. Janie's boyfriend, Lonnie Parris, groundskeeper/maintenance guy for Perkins, picked her up for work every morning at seven-thirty. This particular morning, he shows up, she doesn't answer the door, it's not locked. He comes in, finds her dead, and calls the police. When the cops arrive, Lonnie's gone. Has fled the scene, immediately making him a suspect."

"Why would he call the police? If he's the one who killed her," Stump wonders.

"Back to the facts as stated in these reports. Another question." He looks through photographs. "It's supposedly raining by the time the cops arrive. They're all over the scene. Or should be. You notice anything unusual about that?"

Stump looks at the photographs, and it doesn't take her long to observe. "The carpet. A cream color that shows dirt. It's raining and all these people in and out? Why is the carpet clean?"

"Exactly," Win agrees. "Maybe not as many cops in there as we're supposed to believe? Maybe somebody cleaned up the place just enough to get rid of incriminating evidence? Let's keep going."

"Postmortem took place at a funeral home? That's unusual, too, isn't it?" Stump says.

"Not back then." Flipping a page of his legal pad.

"Cause of death, asphyxiation from being strangled with a ligature, which was the bra tied around her neck." She reads on. "Petechiae of the conjunctivae. Hemorrhage over the back of the larynx and soft tissue over the cervical spine."

"Consistent with strangulation," Win says. "What about other injuries? Bruises, cuts, bite marks, broken fingernails, broken bones, whatever."

Stump scans the report, studies diagrams, says, "Looks like she had bruises around her wrists . . ."

"You mean ligature marks. From her wrists being tied to the chair legs."

"Not just those," Stump says. "It also says there

are marks around her wrists *consistent with fingertip bruises . . .*"

"Suggesting he grabbed her wrists or gripped them tightly." Win keeps making notes. "She struggled with him."

"Not possible they're postmortem? From him dragging the body, moving it when he positioned it?"

"Someone grabbed her wrists while she still had a blood pressure," Win says. "You don't bruise when you're dead."

"Same kind of bruises around her upper arms," Stump says. "And also her hips, buttocks, ankles. It's like everywhere he touched her, it turned into a bruise."

"Keep going. What else?"

"You're right about broken fingernails," she says.

"Defensive. She may have scratched him," Win says. "I hope they swabbed under her nails. Although they didn't do DNA testing back then. But they could have checked for ABO blood types."

The reports are there. Swabs were taken of various orifices. Negative for seminal fluid. Nothing from under her nails, Stump tells him. Maybe they didn't look. Forensic investigations were different back then, to put it mildly.

"What about a tox report?" Win asks, writing in his unique shorthand. Abbreviations and spelling that only he can decipher. "Any mention of alcohol, drugs?"

A few minutes of going through the file and she finds a report from the chemical laboratory on Commonwealth Avenue in Boston. "Negative for drugs and alcohol, although this is interesting." She holds up a police report. "States in the narrative that she was suspected of drug use."

"No drugs in the apartment?" Win frowns. It makes no sense. "What about alcohol in the apartment?"

"Looking," she says.

"Anything on her autopsy report that might indicate she had a history of alcohol abuse, drug abuse?"

"No mention that I can find."

"Then why would someone suggest she might have a history of drug use? What about her trash? Anything found in her trash? What about her medicine cabinet? What was removed from the scene?"

"Here we go," Stump says. "A used syringe with a bent needle in a wastepaper basket. In the bathroom. And in the medicine cabinet, a vial of an unknown substance."

"Certainly the vial must have gone to the lab. The syringe, as well. No report on those?"

"Evidence, evidence . . ." Talking to herself, looking through the files. "Yes, the syringe and vial were submitted. Negative for drugs. Says the vial had, and I quote, 'an oily solution in it with unknown particulate.' "

"Keep going," Win says, writing as fast as he can. "What else was recovered from the scene?"

"Her clothes," Stump reads. "Skirt, blouse, stockings, shoes . . . You can see them in the photos. Her purse, wallet. A keychain with a Saint Christopher's medal—glad he protected her—and two keys. One an apartment key, the other a key to her office at Perkins, it says here. Those things were by the door, on the floor. Dumped out of her purse."

"Let me look again." Win takes all of the

photographs from her, spends some time studying each one.

The scene, the morgue. Nothing he didn't notice earlier, except the scenario is making less sense to him. Her bed was made, and it appears she was dressed for work when she was attacked. A vial found, a used syringe, an unknown substance. Negative drug and alcohol screen.

"Dermatitis on her torso. A rash," Stump reads. "Maybe some sexually transmitted disease? Examination conducted by a Dr. William Hunter, Harvard's Department of Legal Medicine."

"Used to do the medico-legal investigations for the state police," Win says. "Back in the late thirties, the forties. Started by Frances Glessner Lee, this amazing woman into forensics way before her time. Unfortunately, the department she funded doesn't exist anymore."

"You think any of the evidence would still be left?" Stump asks. "Maybe at the Boston ME's office?"

"Wasn't around back then," Win says. "Not until the early eighties. Pathologists at Harvard worked cases as a public service. Any existing records would be at Countway Medical Library at Harvard. But they don't warehouse evidence. And digging around in there could take years."

He looks at photographs taken in Janie Brolin's bedroom. Ransacked drawers, clothing scattered on the floor. Perfume bottles, a hairbrush on top of a dresser, and something else. A pair of dark glasses.

Puzzled, he says, "Why do people who are blind or visually impaired wear dark glasses?"

Stump replies, "I guess to alert others that they're blind. And for self-conscious reasons—to cover their eyes."

"Right. It's not about the weather. About it being sunny," Win says. "I'm not saying that blind eyes aren't sensitive to light, but that's not why blind people wear dark glasses, including indoors. Here." He shows Stump the photograph. "If she were dressed for work, waiting to be picked up, and was ready to go, then why were her dark glasses in her bedroom? Why wasn't she wearing them? Why didn't she have them with her?"

"It was raining, a dark, gloomy day . . ."

"But blind people don't wear dark glasses because of the weather. You just said it yourself," he says.

"Maybe she forgot them for some reason. Maybe she was in the bedroom when someone showed up, interrupted her. Could be a number of reasons."

"Maybe," he says. "Maybe not."

"What are you thinking?"

"I'm thinking we should go get something to eat," Win says.

8

Nine p.m. The FBI's field office in Boston. Special Agent McClure uses the Cyber Task Force's network sniffer to capture Internet traffic of interest.

Specifically, data that fit the profile of e-mail sent from Monique Lamont's IP address and received from another address, also in Cambridge. She's been busy of late, and McClure has to surf through all of her communications, even if they couldn't possibly have anything to do with terrorism and the suspicion she's funding it through a Romanian children's-relief fund that may very well be connected to a nonprofit organization called

FOIL. The FBI is becoming increasingly convinced there's a growing terrorist cell in Cambridge, and Lamont is financially supporting it.

Wouldn't surprise McClure in the least. All those radical students—Harvard, Tufts, MIT—who believe the Constitution ensures that they can do and say pretty much anything they want, even if it's anti-American. For example, holding demonstrations to oppose the war in Iraq, rallying for separation of church and state, disrespecting the flag, and, most personally offensive to the Bureau, vehement attacks on the Patriot Act, which rightly allows the very thing McClure is this moment doing: spying on a private citizen without a court order so other private citizens can be protected from other terrorist attacks or the fear of them. Understandably, there are misfires. Bank accounts, medical records, e-mails, telephone conversations that turn out to be unfortunate violations of people who turn out to have no terrorist involvement whatsoever.

The way McClure views it, however, is that almost everyone who is spied on is guilty of something. Like that John Deere salesman in Iowa a few months back who suddenly came up with enough cash to pay off the fifty thousand dollars he owed various credit-card companies. When his account was automatically flagged, further investigation revealed he had a second cousin whose college roommate's nephew married a woman whose sister's stepdaughter was, for a while, the lesbian lover of a woman whose best friend was a secretary at the Embassy of the Islamic Republic of Iran in Ottawa. Maybe the John Deere salesman wasn't involved in terrorism, but as it turned out, he was buying marijuana allegedly for medical purposes because of alleged nausea due to chemotherapy treatments.

McClure reads an e-mail sent to Lamont in real time.

> I won't withdraw this easily. How can you, after all you've invested in the only true and pure passion you've ever had in your life? Problem is, you want it until it no longer suits, as if it's yours alone to walk away from, and guess what? This time you're into something you can't control. I'm capable of causing destruction that will exceed

anything you could possibly imagine. It's time I show you exactly what I mean. The usual place, tomorrow night at ten. —Me.

Lamont replies.

Okay.

Special Agent McClure forwards the e-mail to Jeremy Killien at Scotland Yard, and writes:

Project FOIL reaching critical mass.

The hell with it, McClure thinks twice. Who cares what time it is over there? Scotland Yard guys can be yanked out of bed the same way FBI agents can. Why should Killien get special consideration? In fact, it would be a pleasure to annoy Detective Superintendent Sherlock. The damn Brits. What have they done except focus on Lamont because of her latest publicity stunt, which caused them to find out she's under investigation, which in turn forced the Bureau to step things up so the Yard doesn't take the credit. It wasn't the Brits who first flagged her as a potential terrorist threat, after all, and now they think they can storm in and steal the Bureau's thunder.

McClure makes the call.

A couple of British-sounding rings, and Killien's sleepy British voice.

"Read your e-mail," McClure says to him.

"Hold on." Not exactly gracious about it.

McClure can hear Killien carrying the portable phone into another room. Hears keys clicking, muttering "damn bloody slow" and "almost got it up. Well, that didn't come out right, did it. There we are. Good God. Don't like the sound of that."

"I think we need to move on it," McClure advises. "Don't see how it can wait. Question's whether you want to be here. On such short notice. I understand it's not . . ."

"No option there," Killien interrupts. "I'll make my arrangements straightaway."

Win apologizes for serving tomatoes that aren't homegrown.

"As if I don't know. I happen to be an expert in

produce," Stump says, sitting some distance from him in his living room. "In fact, you'll probably think this is an awful confession for me to make, but my real job is my market. My father started it from nothing, and it would break his heart if I let him down. But about tomatoes. An insider's tip. Best ones are from Verrill Farm, but we've got a couple months to go, depending on how much rain we get. I love being a cop, but the market loves me back."

The lights are low, his apartment filled with the tantalizing aroma of hickory-smoked bacon. Fresh tomatoes or not, the BLT Win fixed tastes about as good as anything she's ever eaten, and the French Chablis he opened is crisp and clean and perfect. Stump looks out at a typical Cambridge view. Old brick buildings, slate roofs, and lighted windows. When he suggested getting something to eat, she assumed he meant a late-night dinner, was excited and unnerved when he suggested his place. She should have said no. She watches him eating his sandwich and sipping his wine, and feels even more certain that she should have said no. When he lit a candle on the coffee table and turned out the lights, she knew for a fact she'd just made a tactical error.

She sets down her plate, says, "I really should be going."

"Not polite to eat and run."

"You can call me tomorrow if you need more help. But . . ." She starts to get up but seems to be made of stone.

"You're scared of me, aren't you?" he says in the soft, moving light. "Were scared of me long before I got thrown into this case and then pulled you down with me."

"I don't know you. And I tend to be wary of the unfamiliar. Especially if I try to put together pieces and they don't fit."

"What pieces?"

"Where do I start?"

"Wherever you want. Then I'll get to all your pieces that don't fit." His eyes pick up the candlelight.

"I think I need another glass of wine," she says.

"Was just about to do that." He refills their glasses, the leather couch creaking as he moves close.

She smells him, feels his arm barely brushing her sleeve, feels his presence like gravity. Pulling her in.

"Um. Well." Sips her wine. "Start with this. Why do they call you Geronimo?"

"Not sure who *they* are. But why don't you venture a guess. This should be good."

"A mighty warrior. Always on the warpath. Maybe someone who makes potentially fatal leaps. Remember when we were kids? You jump off the high dive and yell 'Geronimo'?"

"Didn't have access to a pool when I was a kid."

"Oh, no. You're not going to give me some discrimination sob story, are you? I happen to know that when you were a kid, people of color were allowed in public schools."

"Didn't say it was about discrimination. I just didn't have access to a pool. The *they* you're talking about is my grandmother. She's the one who nicknamed me Geronimo. Not because of his warrior status or fatal leaps or whatever but because of his eloquence. He said, 'I cannot think that we are useless or God would not have created us. And the sun, the darkness, the winds are all listening to what we have to say.'"

Something catches in her chest. "I don't see the connection," she says.

"Between those words and the person sitting next to you? Maybe I'll tell you, but it's your turn. Why Stump? Honestly speaking? I can't think of any good reason for anybody to call you Stump."

"The World War Two Navy destroyer, USS *Stump*," she says.

"I thought that might be it."

"Seriously. My father came here to escape Mussolini, every horror you can think of when you conjure up that monstrous period of history. One that I hope to hell is never repeated, or I'll believe our entire civilization is damned."

"I worry we're already damned. Worry about it more every day. I'd probably move if there was a good place to run."

"Imagine how the old-timers feel. My dad watches the news three, four hours a day, says he keeps hoping if he watches long enough, things will get better. He's depressed. Sees a psychiatrist. I pay out of pocket because . . . Well, don't get me started on health coverage and all the rest of it. When I was a kid, he started calling me Stump because of the war hero the ship was named after. Admiral Felix Stump, known for his gallantry, his fearlessness. The ship named after him had the motto: 'Tenacity: Foundation of Victory.' My father always said the secret to success is simply not giving up. Kind of a cool thing to tell a little girl."

"When you had your motorcycle accident, didn't it ever occur to you to change your nickname?"

"And how do you do that?" She looks at him, and for reasons she can't fathom, what he just said hurts. "People have called you Stump most of your life and suddenly you tell them, 'Hey, now that half my leg's been amputated, don't call me Stump anymore.' It would be like not calling you Geronimo anymore because you got whacked out and leapt off your balcony or something, paralyzed yourself."

"I'm not reading into this that you might have had suicidal thoughts when you crashed your motorcycle into a guardrail, am I?"

Reaching for her wine, she says, "I don't guess Lamont's ever mentioned my accident. Since she never's really mentioned me, according to you."

"She's never mentioned you, according to her. Never once except the other morning when she said I'd be working with you. Which, by the way, wasn't true at that time, because you had no intention of helping."

"There's good reason why she doesn't talk about me," Stump says. "And there's good reason why she'll probably always regret I didn't die in that accident."

Win is quiet for a moment, looking out the window, drinking his wine. She feels his distance, as if the air between them just got cooler, and anxiety and guilt rush back at her with force. What she's doing is wrong. What she's done is wrong. She gets up from the couch.

"Thanks," she says. "I'd best head out."

He doesn't move. Just stares out the window. The candlelight moving on his profile makes her ache.

"If you need any further help with reports, other paperwork, well, I'm happy to. Anytime," she says.

He turns his head, looks up at her. "What?"

"I'm saying it's not a problem. No big deal." Her feet don't want to move. "You forget who you're talking to." Why doesn't she shut up. "I know when someone has a hard time reading. Another one of those pieces that doesn't fit. Yet one more way you fool people." She's suddenly on the verge of tears. "I don't know why you feel you have to lie about it. To me. I've known it for about as long as I've known you. All those times you come in my shop, ask clever questions to disguise the fact that you can't read the ingredients on a damn jar of marinara sauce . . ."

He stands up, moves close to her, almost menacingly.

"You've got to get past it, that's all," she says, and it crosses her mind that he might hurt her.

Maybe she's goading him into it. Because she deserves it, after what she's done.

"Then both of us are lame," he says.

"That's a terrible word. Don't ever use it around me. Don't ever use it around yourself," she says.

He grips her shoulders, is inches from her face, as if he's about to kiss her, and her heart pounds so hard it throbs in her neck.

"What happened between you and Lamont?" he says. "You asked me the same question. Now I'm asking you."

"It's not what you think."

"How the hell do you know what I think?"

"I know exactly what you think. Exactly what somebody like you would think. All guys like you think about is sex. So if something happens that someone can't talk about, it has to be about sex. Well, what she did to me is about sex, all right."

She pulls him down to the couch, forces his hand on her lower leg, knocks it against her prosthesis, and it makes a hollow sound.

"Don't," he says, almost on top of her, the light of the candle gently shaking the darkness. "Don't do this," he says, sitting up.

"The night we were at Sacco's. She drank at least a bottle of wine by herself, went on about her father, this aristocrat, rich, some internationally prominent lawyer, and how she never meant anything to him and how much she feared it had messed her up, made her act out in ways she didn't really understand and was sorry about later. Well, there's this guy, and he's been staring at her, flirting with her all night. She ends up bringing him back to my house, and they go at it in my bedroom. I'm the one who slept on the couch."

Silence. Win starts rubbing the back of her neck.

"He was this loser, this stupid, crude, ignorant

loser, and as luck would have it, a convicted felon she'd sent to prison a few years earlier. Of course, she didn't remember. All the people who go through her court, so many damn cases you can't remember faces, names. But he remembered her. Which is why he hit on her in the bar to begin with."

"She did something stupid," Win says quietly. "And you were there to see it. Is it really such a big deal?"

"It was to pay her back. To screw her good, as he put it. To screw her worse than she screwed him, he was yelling that morning on his way out my door. Then what does she do? She pulls his case, does a little digging, finds out he's in violation of his parole. Goes back to jail for six months, a year, I don't remember. One day, he and a couple of his redneck buddies see me filling my Harley at a Mobil station on Route Two, follow me, and he starts whooping at me out his window, yelling, making sure I saw his face right before he ran me into the guardrail."

Win pulls her against him, rests his chin on top of her head. "She know?" he asks.

"Oh, sure. Couldn't do anything about it, though, now could we? Or it would come out in court how I first met the guy. How my thinking it was safer to let the two of them have sex in my bedroom instead of her disappearing with some jerk she'd just met in a bar. How my treating her like a friend, in other words, ultimately lost me a leg."

He touches it, traces it with his finger, over her knee, rests his hand on her thigh, says, "It's not about sex. Not the way you mean it. She couldn't ruin that part of you if she tried."

The pathologist who performed the autopsy on Janie Brolin lives on a narrow inlet of the Sudbury River, in an odd little house on an odd property as overgrown as Nana's.

The patio in back is missing bricks and almost completely covered with ivy. An old wooden canoe is stranded in a yard scattered with bright yellow daffodils, violets, and pansies. Win rings the bell, showing up unannounced, and already his day is starting out badly because of good news from the labs. Tracy found prints.

His idea of trying luminol paid off in one respect—a latent print fluoresced on the disposable camera package he found in the Victorian mansion, meaning whoever touched the cardboard had a copper residue on at least one of his fingers. Copper and blood both fluoresce when sprayed with luminol, a common crime scene problem that in this instance worked to Win's advantage. Unfortunately, the copper-residue print doesn't match anyone in the AFIS database. As for other prints? The ones on the wine bottle came back to Stump and Win, and as for Farouk, he left several partials on the envelope he touched. The Fresca can and note from Raggedy Ann both have prints that match one another but don't match anybody in AFIS, either.

Stump lied.

Now's not the time to think about it, he tells himself as he rings Dr. Hunter's doorbell again.

How could she? In his arms, in his bed, staying with him until four a.m. He just made love to a lie.

"Who is it?"

Win identifies himself as state police.

"Come around to the window and give me proof," a strong voice says through the door.

Win moves to one side of the porch, holds his credentials up to the glass. An old man in a three-wheel mini-scooter peers at the creds, then at Win, seems satisfied, drives back to the door, and lets him in.

"Safe as it is around here, I've seen too much. Wouldn't trust a girl scout," Dr. Hunter says, driving into a wormy chestnut living room that overlooks the water. On a desk is a computer and a router, piles of books and papers.

He parks across from the fireplace, and Win sits on the hearth, looking around at photographs, many of them younger versions of Dr. Hunter with a pretty woman who Win supposes was his wife. A lot of happy moments with family, friends, a framed newspaper story with a black-and-white picture of Dr. Hunter at a crime scene, police everywhere.

"I have a feeling I know why you're here," Dr. Hunter says. "That old murder case suddenly in the news. Janie Brolin. Must say, I couldn't believe it when I first heard. Why now? Then, of course, our friendly local DA is known for, shall we say, her surprises."

"Ever enter your mind way back then that the Boston Strangler did it?"

"Utter nonsense. Women raped and strangled with their own clothing, their bodies displayed, and all the rest? It's one thing to use a scarf or stockings and tie them in a bow, quite another to use the victim's bra, which in my experience usually happens when the killer was sexually assaulting her, shoving and tearing at her clothing, and the bra is the most obvious and convenient ligature because of its general vicinity to the neck. I should add that Janie wasn't the sort to let anybody in her house for any reason whatsoever unless she was absolutely certain who it was."

"Because she was blind," Win supposes.

"I'm not far from it myself. Macular degeneration," he says. "But I can tell a lot by a person's voice. More than I used to. When one of your senses gets worse, the others pitch in and try to help it out. Journalists were more circumspect in 1962, or maybe her family just wouldn't talk or the press wasn't interested. I don't know, but what was left out of the papers, as best I recall, was Janie Brolin's father was a doctor in London's East End and no stranger to crime, patched up victims of it on a regular basis. Her mother worked in a pharmacy that had been robbed a couple of times."

"So Janie wasn't naïve," Win says.

"Feisty, street-smart, which is one of the reasons she had the pluck to take a year abroad, all by herself, and come to Watertown."

"Because of Perkins. She was blind and wanted to work with the blind."

"That's the speculation."

"You ever talk with her family?"

"Her father, just once and very briefly. As you well know, not everybody wants to talk to the pathologist. They can't deal with our part in it, mainly ask the same question time after time."

"If their loved one suffered."

"That's it," Dr. Hunter says. "Rather much the only thing her father asked me. He wanted a copy of the death certificate but not the autopsy report. Neither he nor his wife came over here. The body was returned to London along with what few personal effects she had. But he didn't want to know the details."

"Unusual for a doctor."

"Not for a father."

"What did you say when he asked?"

"I said she suffered. I never lied. You can't lie."

Stump enters Win's mind.

"You tell someone what he wants to hear, that his loved one didn't suffer, and then what happens if the case goes to court and the defense finds out you said that?" Dr. Hunter says. "He catches you in a lie—albeit a well-intended one. And your credibility's impeached. Now, then. I'll give you what I've got. Isn't much."

His chair quietly hums as he drives toward a doorway. "Dug up what I could find when I heard about all this on the news. Figured somebody was going to ask, and I figured right." In the hallway. "All this mess in my closets, under beds . . ." Fades out. Then comes back. "A few things from those days because we knew better back then."

He parks his scooter, a Bankers Box on his lap, keeps talking. "In the first place. Harvard really wasn't all that gung-ho about having a department of legal medicine or they'd still have one. There were a few of us pathologists who liked the investigative part, were only too happy to do autopsies, be crime doctors, as some people called us. But we held on to our own records, to whatever we deemed important or wanted to use for teaching purposes, knowing full well that when we went out the door, there wasn't going to be anybody left who gave a damn about our legacy. By the way. You see her on YouTube?"

Lamont. Which makes Win think of Stump again.

"Can't believe what people do these days," Dr. Hunter says. "Glad I'm not your age. Happy to be trekking along on the downslope. Not much to look forward to except home movies made by strangers, and, well . . . one of my granddaughters's in Iraq. And I'm supposed to be in a retirement home with a lot of my friends, those left, anyway. Been on the list five years, my number recently came up. Can't afford it because I can't sell my house. Not so long ago, people were fighting over it." He indicates the computer on his desk overlooking the river. "I call it a cyber-pandemic. Once the floodgate opens, and you know the rest."

"I'm sorry . . ."

"Monique Lamont, I mean. The second one's

worse than the first. Go log on." A wave of his hand, indicating the computer again. "I get Google alerts for all sorts of things. The DA, crime, city council, because I like to keep up with what's going on in Middlesex County. Since I happen to live in it."

Win goes over to the computer, logs on to the Internet, doesn't take him long to find the latest video clip making the rounds.

The Commodores singing, "Ow, she's a brick house . . ." As Lamont in a hard hat, other officials, and construction workers inspect tons of collapsed concrete ceiling slabs inside a tunnel near Boston's Logan Airport.

Then a voice-over from one of her old campaign ads: "Getting to the bottom of it, demanding justice." As Lamont stoops over, inspects a section of a twisted steel tieback, her fitted skirt hikes up to her buttocks.

Dr. Hunter says, "Obviously, from that road construction disaster last summer, the Big Dig, when that tunnel collapsed and crushed that car, killed the woman passenger. Never was a fan of Monique Lamont, but now I'm starting to feel sorry for her.

It's not right to do that to somebody. But that's not why you're here. If I knew the answer to Janie Brolin, the case would have been solved when I was working it. My opinion now is the same as it was. A domestic homicide staged to look like a sexual homicide."

"Staged by her boyfriend. Lonnie Parris?"

"They'd been heard arguing in the past, if my memory serves me well. Reports from neighbors of the two of them going at each other. So that morning, maybe he comes to pick her up for work. They get into it. He strangles her, then stages it to look like some sexual predator did it. Flees the scene and has the misfortune of having a close encounter of the vehicular kind."

"All I found about him was a newspaper article, couldn't find his case file. Assume Cambridge has it, since it was a Cambridge case. Did you do his autopsy?"

"I did. Multiple trauma. What you'd expect if you were run over."

"Run over? As opposed to being struck while you're upright?"

"Oh, he was run over, for sure. More than once.

Some of his injuries were postmortem, indicating to me he'd been dead on the road for a while, long enough for a couple more cars to run over him before somebody finally felt a bump, decided it might be a good idea to get out and check. This was early in the morning. Dark out."

"Possible he might already have been dead before he was run over?"

"You mean staged to look like an accident? It's possible. All I can tell you is he wasn't stabbed and he wasn't shot. He certainly suffered massive trauma, especially to his head, while he was alive."

"I just find it interesting that he called the police from Janie's apartment after supposedly walking in and finding her murdered," Win says. "Then he disappears before the police show up. And not even twenty-four hours later, he's dead in the middle of a road. Not hit while he was standing. But run over because he was already on the pavement."

"We did the best we could. Didn't have the wizardry you do these days."

"We don't have wizardry, but certainly there are capabilities that didn't exist when you were working these cases, Dr. Hunter. I'm wondering"—pointing at the Bankers Box—"what you've got."

"Mostly the same old records in here you've probably already seen. The Cambridge records included. But the best stuff—well, it would have been somewhat unseemly for me to walk out the door with it when I retired. Specifically, pathological specimens. When the Department of Legal Medicine was disbanded in the eighties, our specimens stayed behind, no doubt were thrown out eventually. I wish I still had Janie Brolin's eyes. Quite fascinating. Used to pass them around in wet labs. It was anybody's guess."

"What about her eyes?" Win asks.

"As you might expect, during her autopsy, I shone a bright light into her eyes, wondering if I might discover anything on gross examination that would account for her blindness. And I discovered strange shiny brownish specks over the corneas, what I suspect was the sequela of a disease process that caused her blindness. Or maybe she was suffering from some undiagnosed neurological degeneration that might result in an altered distribution of pigmentation. To this day, don't know.

Well, not useful for your purposes, anyway. A medical curiosity that's more to my taste."

"May I?" Win gets up, walks over to the Bankers Box.

"Be my guest."

Win carries it back to the hearth, takes off the lid. The expected paperwork and photographs, and a plastic airtight food container.

"Been around a long time, hasn't it?" Dr. Hunter says. "Tupperware. That and Ball glass jars. Staples in the morgue."

The lid is labeled with the case number that by now is so familiar: WT218–62. Inside are a syringe with a bent needle and a small vial that Win holds up to the light.

An oily residue in it, and what looks like tiny flecks of tarnished copper.

9

After a quick stop at the labs to drop off the syringe and vial, he checks on Nana.

"Brought your car back," he says loudly. "Door unlocked. Alarm off. At least I can take some comfort in consistency. Because everything else is chaos, Nana."

All this as he carries groceries into her kitchen, not realizing she has a visitor. Poor Mrs. Murphy from Salem. Quite the irony that Nana has clients from what is literally called "The Witch City," where the police department emblem features a witch flying on a broom. No joke.

"I didn't realize you were with someone." He sets down the bags, starts putting things away.

Groceries from a real grocery store, where he paid full price.

"How you doing, Mrs. Murphy?" he asks.

"Oh, not so good."

"Looks to me like you've lost some weight."

"Oh, not so much." The ever-morose Mrs. Murphy, all three hundred pounds of her.

Has a glandular condition, she says. It's no better, she says. Does everything Nana tells her, and for a while, not so bad. Then the psychic vampire shows up again, drains her life force while she's asleep, and she's too depressed and tired to exercise or to do anything but eat.

"I know," Win says. "I work for a psychic vampire. It's hell."

Mrs. Murphy laughs, slapping her huge thighs. "You're such a funny one. Always cheer me up," she says. "I told you to get away from her, though. You seen her movies? Oh, whatever they're called. Same thing the presidential candidates are doing. You-Two or something. Anyway, I keep up with you and that big case you're suddenly doing. I remember that case, don't you?" Nodding at Nana. "It was like someone doing that to Helen Keller when she was young, only, of course, nobody killed Helen Keller. Thank God."

"Thank God," Nana agrees.

"I remember thinking it was like Alfred Hitchcock. Not an original thought. A lot of people said that at the time. Sort of like *Wait Until Dark*, where you imagine this poor blind girl struggling to dial the phone, struggling to get help, and she can't even see the phone, much less the killer. Not knowing which direction to run because she can't see anything. How terrifying is that? Well, I'll be going so you can spend some time with your boy," Mrs. Murphy says to Nana.

Win helps Mrs. Murphy out of her chair.

"Such the gentleman, that one." She opens her pocketbook, pulls out a twenty-dollar bill, leaves it on the table, points her finger at Win. "I still got that daughter of mine, you know. Lilly's a fine one—and not dating anybody at the moment."

"I'm so busy right now, I'm not fit for a lady, especially one as fine as your daughter."

"Such a gentleman." She says it again, enters a number on her cell phone, says to whoever answers,

"I'm coming out now. What? Oh, no. It's better if I wait in the driveway. I'm too tired to walk around the block, honey."

She leaves, and Nana opens the refrigerator, takes a look at what Win just bought.

"All sorts of wonderful things, my darling," she says, opening a cupboard, checking in there, too. "What's happened with your friend?"

"It was easier to stop at Whole Foods. That roasted chicken is right off the rotisserie, and the wild rice salad—you need some grain. Has nuts and dried cranberries. I filled your car with gas, checked the oil, you're all set."

"Sit down for a minute," Nana says. "See this?" Points to a large gold locket she's wearing around her neck, one of about ten other chains with charms and symbols he doesn't understand. "I have a piece of your hair in this locket from when you were a baby. And now I've added a piece of my hair. Maternal energy, my darling. Your grandmother protecting her grandson. There are angels walking the earth. Don't you fear."

"If you run into one, send her my way." He smiles at her.

"What happened with your friend?"

"What friend, and what makes you think anything happened?"

"The one who's caused a darkness in your heart. It's not what you think it is."

"Nothing's ever what I think it is," he says. "That's what makes life interesting, right? Gotta go."

"England," she says.

He stops in the doorway. "That's right. Janie Brolin was from England." It's been all over the news.

Lamont and Scotland Yard, the dynamic duo. Who knows? Maybe they'll save what's left of the world.

"No," Nana says emphatically. "It's not about that poor girl."

Outside, he puts on his motorcycle gear while Mrs. Murphy watches, her big fake-leather pocketbook looped over the crook of a corpulent arm.

"You look like one of those shows," she says. "*Star Trek.* I used to love Captain Kirk. Now he does those travel commercials. Isn't that an irony? Captain Kirk doing travel commercials, I guess staying in hotels where *no man's stayed before.*" Laughing. "For ninety-nine dollars. Nobody sees the irony except me."

Win puts on his helmet, says, "You want to hop on the back and I'll give you a ride?"

She guffaws. "Don't make me wet my pants! My Lord in heaven. A whale like me on a itty-bitty jet ski."

"Come on." He pats the back of the seat. "Hop on. I'll take you to your car."

Her face goes slack. Then something soft and sad in her eyes, because he means it.

"Well, there's Ernie," she says as a Toyota turns into the driveway.

Lamont's in her office when he gets off the elevator.

Doesn't take a detective to figure that out. Her car's in its reserved parking place, her office door's shut, and he can hear the faint murmur of voices behind it. She's probably talking to her latest Ken-doll press secretary. Win walks into the investigative unit, barely speaks to his colleagues, who give him a curious look, since he's supposed to be on leave solving a case of international importance. Mainly what he needs right now is his comfort zone, his phone, and his computer. He sets Dr. Hunter's files on the desk, checks his grandfather's allegedly stolen watch. It's almost nine p.m. in London. He goes on the Internet, finds a general information number for Scotland Yard, tells the lady who answers he's a homicide detective in Massachusetts and really needs to speak to the commissioner. It's urgent.

That goes over like the proverbial lead balloon. Sort of like calling the White House and asking for the president. After much to-do, he gets a pleasant enough woman in the investigative division, finds out the man he wants is Detective Superintendent Jeremy Killien. Problem is, he's out of the country.

"You know where he can be reached?"

"Left for the United States. That's all I know. If you call back tomorrow during office hours, perhaps one of the commissioner's administrative assistants can be of service." She gives him a direct number.

Can't be about the Brolin case. No way some

detective superintendent from Scotland Yard would be flying all the way here about that. Win sits and thinks, shakes three Advils from a bottle, has a wicked headache and that detached, slow-motion feeling he gets when he's sleep-deprived, not working out or eating enough. He starts on Dr. Hunter's files, most of what's in them the same information he and Stump looked at in the records room. Well, he's not going to ask her to help him with anything now, and he goes through notes, other paperwork, sentence by sentence, page by page, comes across a name that stops him cold.

J. Edgar Hoover.

Other names, Mafia names that are vaguely familiar, scribbles in Dr. Hunter's almost unreadable hand, sketchy references to a conversation he had on April 10 with a journalist who worked for the Associated Press. Win logs on to the Internet, initiates one search after another. The reporter won several awards for a number of series he wrote about organized crime. Win starts printing out stories. Reading them is slow going, and, as he expected, the journalist died years ago, so forget talking to him.

At almost five p.m., his phone rings.

It's Tracy from the labs.

"Nothing helpful from DNA. No matches in CODIS. But you were right," she says.

He asked her to take samples from the syringe and vial, and to examine them with the scanning electron microscope and X-ray analysis so they could magnify the particulate in the oily residue and also determine its elemental composition. Assuming the strange brownish flecks are inorganic—like copper.

"They're metal," she confirms.

"What the hell would have copper in it? She was injecting particles of copper into herself?"

"Not copper," Tracy says. "Gold."

What begins to emerge is a portrait of a violent tragedy that, like almost all others Win has worked, is rooted in randomness, bad timing, a seemingly insignificant incident that ends a person's life in an astonishingly brutal way.

Although he'll never prove it, because there's no one left to say, it appears that less than forty-eight hours before Janie Brolin was murdered, she set the fatal event in motion by the simple act of stepping outside her apartment door to continue an argument with her boyfriend, Lonnie Parris. Win gets up from his desk, realizes he's been at it for almost five hours. He passes empty cubicle after empty cubicle, everyone gone. On the other side of the floor are the district attorney's offices, and the door to Lamont's suite. She's there. He can feel her intense, selfish energy. He knocks, doesn't wait for an answer, walks in, shuts the door behind him.

She's standing behind her spotless glass desk, packing her briefcase, looks up at him, an uneasy expression flitting across her face. Then she's her inscrutable self again, in a smoky blue suit and a greenish-black blouse, a subtle mismatch that is so Armani.

Win helps himself to a chair, says, "I need a few minutes."

"I don't have them." Shutting her briefcase, loud snaps as she fastens the clasps.

"I think you might want the information before I pass it along to Scotland Yard, to Jeremy Killien. And by the way, when you recruit other agencies into my investigation, it would be polite to let me know."

She sits, says, "You're well aware the Yard's involved."

"Right, now I am. Because I heard about it in the news you leaked."

"I didn't leak it. The governor did."

"Gee. Wonder how he found out. Maybe someone leaked it to him first."

"We're not discussing this," she says, as only she can. Never a comment, always a command. "Obviously, you have news about our case. Good news, I hope?"

"I don't think anything about this case could be good news. For you, it's probably not good news, and if Jeremy Killien weren't on his way to the US or already here, I'd advise you to let him know he probably doesn't need to waste Scotland Yard's time on . . ."

"He's on his way here? And how might you know that?"

"One of his colleagues told me. He left for the States. Don't know when and don't know why."

"Must be for some other reason. Not because of

our case." She doesn't sound so sure of that. "I can't imagine him coming here and not discussing it with me first."

She switches on an art glass lamp, the window behind her dark. Lights in surrounding buildings are blurred by fog. It's going to rain, and Lamont hates rain. Hates it so much he once suggested she might have a seasonal affective disorder. One Christmas he even bought her a light box that's supposed to mimic the sun and lift your mood. Didn't work. Annoyed the hell out of her. Bad weather is bad timing for bad news.

"Janie Brolin most likely suffered from rheumatoid arthritis, probably had since she was a child," Win begins. "Maybe because her father was a doctor, it seems she resorted to a rather innovative treatment of sodium aurothiomalate. You familiar?"

"No." Impatiently, as if she's got someplace to go and is uptight about it.

"Gold salts. Used to threat chronic arthritis. Hard to say what dosage. Could have been ten to fifty milligrams weekly. Could have been less at longer intervals, administered by injection. Possible side effects include blood disorders, dermatitis, a proclivity to bruise easily—which might explain the excessive bruising all over her body. Plus corneal chrysiasis . . ."

Lamont shrugs, one of her "you've lost me" looks. Her way of treating him as if she's bored and he's stupid. She's getting more tense by the moment, intermittently glancing up at the Venetian glass clock on the wall across from her desk.

"Gold deposits in the corneas, which don't cause visual disturbances—in other words, don't impair your vision. But upon examination with a light, you see these minute brownish metallic flecks. What she had on autopsy," Win says.

"So what?"

"So everything adds up to her not being blind but having photosensitivity, another possible side effect from gold therapy. And people with sensitivity to light tend to wear dark glasses."

"And so what?"

"And so she wasn't blind."

"And so what?"

"And you just don't want to hear it, do you?"

"Hear your tangled thoughts? I don't have time to work my way through them."

"I believe Janie Brolin was a Mob hit. As was her boyfriend, Lonnie Parris. Her apartment was in the heart of Watertown's Mafiaville. She was fully aware of what was going on around her because she wasn't blind, meaning she sure as hell would have seen who was at her door the morning of April fourth, meaning it probably was someone she trusted enough to let in. Not necessarily her boyfriend, Lonnie Parris, who no more murdered her than the Boston friggin' Strangler did. I think by the time Lonnie showed up to drive her to Perkins, she was already dead. He walked in and found her."

Lamont says, "I'm waiting for whatever you're basing all of your assumptions on. In fact, I'm waiting for any of this to make sense."

"Two days earlier. April second," Win says. "A Mob underboss who happened to live across the street from Janie used contacts at the Registry of Motor Vehicles to get a license plate run so he could get the address of a certain juror who was a holdout in a not-guilty verdict. One of the underboss's boys was on trial for murder. In addition to being unhelpful, this juror also made an unfortunate comment, insulted this same underboss. Look it up. Plenty was written about it in the press."

Lamont. That stare of hers. As unwavering as a cat's.

"The inappropriate remark implied this Mob underboss and J. Edgar Hoover had a ménage à trois with another high-ranking FBI official. By the way, not that such things hadn't been said before. But in this instance, the underboss in question—Janie's neighbor—had a couple of his guys show up at the juror's residence, abducted him, brought him back to the underboss's house. Not about persuading him to change his mind as much as it was about revenge. He ends up dead. His body goes in the car trunk, never to be seen again. That much is known from other cases later on, subsequent testimony from informants, et cetera."

"And has to do with what?"

"Has to do with the fact that on that particular night, April second, according to notes I've come across, various reports, and so on, Janie and her boyfriend were heard arguing in her apartment. This argument led outside, culminating in his storming off in his car."

"Maybe I'm just obtuse," Lamont says.

"She was home the night the juror was murdered across the damn street and loaded in a car trunk, Monique. And she wasn't blind. And anybody who knew her would have been aware of that. We'll probably never know exactly what happened, but it's more than possible that on the morning of April fourth, one of the Mob guys showed up at her place. Probably a neighbor, someone she was acquainted with. She opens her door, and that's it. Murdered, staged to look like a sexual homicide and a burglary. Without knowing he's part of the scenario, Lonnie shows up, walks in, makes this horrible discovery, calls the police. Boom. Mob guys show up, grab him, and off he goes."

"Why?"

"He probably saw the same thing Janie saw on April second. He was a liability. Or a scapegoat. Make it look as if he killed her and fled, and then accidentally gets hit by a car. Problem is, he wasn't hit. He was run over. How did that happen? He pass out while crossing the street in the early-morning hours after Janie was killed?"

"Drunk?"

"Tox was negative for drugs and alcohol. Good plan. Her death is explained. His death is explained. The end."

"The end? That's it?"

"That's it. Your Boston Strangler theory? As much as it breaks my heart? Forget it. Better call the governor. Better call the Yard. Better call a press conference. Since your international case has already been in the news from here to the moon. And England's got nothing to do with this except it lost a nice young woman to some Mafia dirtbags who happened to be her neighbors while she was enjoying a year in the States. She would have been better off blind."

"And that never came out at the time of the investigation? That she wasn't really blind?" Lamont asks.

"People make assumptions. Maybe nobody asked or cared or thought it was relevant. And then there's the cover-up factor. The police obviously cooperating with the Mob, since it appears that's what this is about."

"If she wasn't blind, why the hell would she work with them?" Lamont asks.

"The blind, I assume you mean."

"Why? If she wasn't?"

"She had a disease that caused her suffering every day. Changed her life. Limited it in some ways. Made her try harder, more courageous, too. Miracles and the Midas Touch. And nothing really worked. Why wouldn't she care about the pain and suffering of others?"

"Wasn't worth it. That's for damn sure," Lamont says. "Still a big story. It's all about how you spin it. Let's don't be coy. Better it doesn't come from a press release or press conference, which nobody really trusts, the public doesn't. Especially these days." She smiles as her next brainstorm hits. "A college reporter."

"You're not serious."

"Perfect. Absolutely serious," she says, getting up, grabbing her briefcase. "Not from me but from you. I want you to get with Cal Tradd."

"You're going to place a story like this in the friggin' *Crimson*? A student newspaper?"

"He investigated it, worked with you, with us, and what a great story. Becomes a story about a story. Just the sort of thing people love with this 'everybody's a journalist, everybody's the star in his own movie' craze. Reality TV, YouTube. Average Joe saves the day. Yes, indeed. And, of course, the general media will pick it up, will go all over the place, and everybody's happy."

Win walks out after her, slides his iPhone off his belt, remembers the piece of paper in his wallet. Gets it out, unfolds it, is entering Cal's cell phone number when he notices something as the elevator doors close, taking Lamont down to the lower level of the courthouse, to her car. He holds up the piece of white notepaper, tilts it this way and that, can barely see indented letters, the faintest shadow behind the telephone numbers Cal wrote in a very neat hand.

A *T,* and *AG,* and what looks like a *W* followed by an exclamation point. He runs back into his office, grabs a sheet of printing paper, a pencil, remembering his conversation with Stump inside the mobile crime lab, their examination of the note used in the most recent bank robbery. A note exactly like three others in three earlier bank robberies. Neatly written in pencil on a four- by six-inch sheet of white paper, and he uses a ruler, draws a rectangle four by six inches—same size as the piece of paper Cal gave him. Win works it out, lining up the indented letters with what he remembers about the bank robbery note Stump showed him.

EMPTY CASH DRAWER IN BAG. NOW! I HAVE A GUN.

The image on the surveillance tape. The robber was about Cal's height but looked heavier. No problem. Wear several layers of clothes under your baggy warm-up suit. Darker skin. Dark hair. A million ways to do that. Including mascara—oldest trick in the book, and washes off in minutes. A quick search of the National Criminal Information Center, NCIC. Cal Tradd. His date of birth and absence of a criminal record, explaining why there are no prints or DNA on file—not that he's ever left either, it would seem, except, perhaps, a coppery print on a disposable camera package that luminol reacted to as if the print were left in blood.

Bank robberies and copper thefts from all over this area. Excluding Cambridge, where Cal goes to school. And Boston, where he's from, Win thinks.

He tries Lamont, and his call rolls over to voice mail on the first ring. Either on the phone or she has it turned off. He tries Stump. Same thing. He doesn't leave a message for either one of them as he runs out of the courthouse, grabs his motorcycle gear out of the hard case, speeds off. A light rain smacks his face shield and makes the pavement slick as he weaves in and out of traffic toward Cambridge.

10

Lamont's car is in the driveway of the Victorian ruin on Brattle Street, not a single light on, no sign of anyone.

Win touches the hood of her Mercedes. It's warm, and he notes the quiet clicking sound car engines usually make right after they've been turned off. He goes around to the side of the house, out of sight, waiting, listening. Nothing. Minutes pass. Every window is dark, has nothing to do with the candle he took from the room where he found the mattress, the wine. Something else is going on, he can tell by looking through the window he broke the other night. The alarm panel is dead, no green light. He walks around, looking for cut power lines, for any indication of why there might be an electrical failure. Nothing, and he returns to the back door.

It's unlocked, and he opens it, hears footsteps on the wooden flooring. The impatient flipping of switches. Someone walking room to room. Switches flipping. Win shuts the door behind him, loudly, so whoever it is—Lamont, he's sure—will know someone has just come in.

Footsteps head his way, and Lamont calls out, "Cal?"

Win walks toward her voice.

"Cal?" she calls out again. "There are no lights anywhere. What happened to the lights? Where are you?"

A switch flipping on and off in the room beyond the kitchen, what may once have been a dining room. Win turns on his tactical light and shines it obliquely so he doesn't blind her.

"It's not Cal," he says, directing the light at a wall, illuminating the two of them.

They're standing maybe six feet apart in the

middle of an empty, cavernous room with old wooden flooring and ornate molding.

"What are you doing here!" she exclaims.

He turns the light off. Complete darkness.

"What are you doing!" She sounds scared.

"Shhhh," he says, moves toward her, finds her arm. "Where is he?"

"Let go of me!"

He leads her to the wall, whispers for her to stand right there. Don't move. Don't make a sound, then he waits by the doorway, no more than ten feet from her, but it seems to be miles. He waits for Cal. Long, tense minutes, and a noise. The back door opens. The beam of a flashlight enters the room before the person does, and then confusion as Win grabs someone, a struggle, and footsteps from all directions, and Stump is yelling, and then nothing.

"Are you all right?"

"Win?"

"Win?"

He opens his eyes, and the lights are on in the house, and Raggedy Ann is standing over him. Dressed a little differently this time. In a polo shirt, cargo pants, a pistol on her hip. Stump, Lamont, and some big guy in a suit, thick, gray hair.

"It's my damn house. I have every right to be here," Lamont is saying.

Win's head hurts like hell. He touches a huge lump on it, looks at blood on his hand.

"An ambulance is on the way," Stump says, crouching next to him.

He sits up, sees black for an instant, says, "You hit me, or do I have someone else to thank."

"That would be me," Raggedy Ann says.

She introduces herself as Special Agent McClure, FBI. The big guy in the suit is New Scotland Yard's Jeremy Killien. Now that Win knows the complete cast of characters, he suggests they might want to broadcast a "Be on the Lookout," a BOLO, for Cal Tradd. Since he's probably a bank robber, and a copper thief, and his luring the district attorney here was for purposes of blackmail, bribery, threatening her. Monique and Win set the whole thing up. All part of a sting operation that just got blown to hell. Lamont watches him spin the story. Not a glint of gratitude in her eyes that he's saving her ass.

"What sting operation?" McClure asks, baffled.

Win rubs his head, says, "Monique and I have been on this guy for a while. The way he follows me around, then started following her around, not to mention his maniacal obsession with covering the very crimes we were suspicious he was committing. Typical sociopathic behavior. This seventeen-year-old whiz kid—well, actually sixteen, birthday's next month—sheltered and controlled all his life, until he finally left home for college, younger than the usual freshman."

Nothing registers on Lamont's face. But Win has no doubt she didn't know. Even she wouldn't stoop so low as to have sex with a minor, if that's what the two of them have been doing when they rendezvoused in the very house Cal probably vandalized, stripped of copper. Then photographed. For souvenirs, just as he's done at so many other places. Thrill crimes. Not because he needs the money. Imagine that. Super Thief. Reporting on your own copper thefts and bank robberies, getting chummy with the very people investigating your crimes, even screwing the district attorney. What a wunderkind.

"This is completely embarrassing," Killien says in disgust.

"Whose bright idea was it to have the power turned off?" Win looks at McClure. "Oh. You guys. The F-Big-I. Then what?" Rubbing his head. "You call the power company and have it turned back on? Pretty cool to have connections like that. No pun intended." To Stump. "I don't need an ambulance." Touching the knot on his head again. "Fact is, I feel smarter. Isn't it true some people who get hit on the head with a flashlight end up with a higher IQ?"

"What sting operation?" Stump isn't amused.

No one is. Everybody looking at him with hard faces.

"You never mentioned any sting operation to me," Stump says.

"Well, you weren't exactly forthright with me, either. At least not about Special Agent Raggedy Ann."

"It's McClure," says the FBI agent.

"A print on a Fresca can," Win says to Stump. "A print on a note delivered to my apartment. No hit in AFIS, meaning the person who left them sure as hell didn't spend time in prison for stabbing her pimp. Sure as hell has no arrest record at all. And now that I know she's FBI, some undercover whatever, I'm not surprised she has no prints on file for exclusionary purposes."

"I couldn't tell you," Stump says.

"I get it," Win says. "Of course, you couldn't tell me that this Raggedy Ann criminal was really an informant who is really an FBI agent who is spying on me because she's really spying on Lamont."

"I believe you should lie back down," Killien says to him.

Stump continues to explain. "When you were so determined to follow her, Win, I had to come up with the Filippello Park scenario, have her deliver the note and all the rest. So it would appear I had no choice but to admit she was an informant, ensuring you would back off before you figured out she's FBI. You know how it works. We don't give up our informants, and had I offered that information easily, you would have been suspicious. So I had to script something. I had to make it appear I had no choice but to blow her cover and order you to stay the hell away from her."

They hold each other's gaze for a moment.

"I'm sorry," Stump says.

"So why the party?" Win says to everyone. "Why are we here? Because it's not about Janie Brolin. And it's not about Cal Tradd."

"I believe the easy answer is we're here because of your district attorney," Killien says to Lamont. "Romanian orphans. Large transfers of cash. Which flagged you, brought you to the attention of the FBI, Homeland Security. Finally, the Yard, unfortunately."

"What I should do is sue the hell out of every last one of you," she says.

And McClure says to her, "Your electronic communications with . . ."

"With Cal." Lamont steps into a role no one plays better than she does. The DA again. "I think Investigator Garano's made it clear what we've been doing since these serial bank robberies, copper thefts began here in Middlesex County. That part of our sting operation was my communicating with Cal, who's been, to put it mildly, of interest."

"You knew she was e-mailing Cal Tradd?" Stump asks McClure.

"No. We didn't know who she was e-mailing.

The IP came back to Harvard. A machine code isn't helpful unless you can find the machine to compare it . . ."

"I know how it works." The look on Stump's face.

She probably liked McClure better when she was Raggedy Ann.

"The most recent e-mail indicating you would be meeting this person of interest . . ." McClure starts to say.

"Cal," Lamont says. "Meet him in the usual place at ten. Meaning here at ten."

"He didn't turn up," Killien says.

"Probably saw a posse thundering on the horizon and scuttled away," Win says. "The kid's used to dodging cops. Has cop radar. So you guys show up and blow everything Monique and I have been working on for months. And that's the problem when you monitor electronic communications, now, isn't it? Especially when you're undercover and monitoring somebody else who's undercover, one sting operation investigating what turns out to be another sting operation, and everybody gets stung."

*

Two nights later, the Harvard Faculty Club.

Georgian Revival brick, oil portraits on mahogany-paneled walls, brass chandeliers, Persian rugs, the usual arrangement of fresh flowers in the entryway—so familiar and intended to make him feel out of place. No fault of Harvard's, just another Lamontism. She always summons him to the faculty club when she needs to feel powerful, or more powerful than usual, because she either is secretly insecure or needs him, or both.

Win sits on the same stiff antique sofa he always sits on, the tick-tock of a grandfather clock reminding him Lamont's one minute late, two minutes, three, ten. He watches people come and go, all these academicians, visiting dignitaries and lecturers, or prominent families visiting to investigate whether they should send their prominent children here. One thing he loves about Harvard, it's like a priceless work of art. You never own it. You never deserve it. You just get to visit it for a while, and are a far better person for the association, even if it doesn't remember you. Probably was never even aware of you. That's what he finds sad about Lamont, no matter how much he dislikes her at times, finds her despicable at times.

What she has will never be enough.

She walks in, furling her umbrella, shaking rain off her coat as she slips out of it, heading to the cloakroom.

"You ever notice it always rains when we meet here?" Win asks her as they walk into the dining room, sit at their usual table by a window overlooking Quincy Street.

"I need a drink," she says. "How about you?" A tight smile, scant eye contact.

This can't be easy for her, and she searches for the waiter, decides it might be nice to have a bottle of wine. White or red? Win says either.

"Why did you do it?" Smoothing her linen napkin in her lap, reaching for her water. "We both know, and for the record, this conversation not only will never happen again, but it didn't happen at all."

"Then why bother?" he says. "Why did you invite me to dinner if all you wanted was to talk about not talking and exact the promise that we'd never talk about not talking again? Or whatever you just said."

"I'm in no mood to be glib."

"Then fire away. I'm listening."

"Foundation of International Law," she says. "My father's foundation."

"I believe all of us know what FOIL is by now. Or what you turned it into. A limited liability company, a front to protect and shield the person behind the purchase of a multimillion-dollar Victorian ruin that will take years to renovate. Too bad you didn't pick some other name, can't help but wonder about the karma of using a name associated with a father who always treated you like . . ."

"I really don't think you're in a position to discuss my father."

The waiter arrives with a silver bucket of ice, a fine bottle of Montrachet. He uncorks it. Lamont tastes it. Two glasses filled, waiter gone, and Lamont starts looking at the menu.

"I can't remember what you usually get here." She changes the subject.

Win retrieves it. "More than anyone you know, I'm in a position to discuss your father. Because at the end of the day, Monique, he's why you got yourself into a mess that could have . . ."

"I don't need to hear your version of what it

could have done." Drinking her wine. "Are you really surprised I'd buy another house? Maybe not want to live in the same one? Maybe spend very little time there. Almost none. Actually, I rented an apartment at the Ritz, but driving back and forth from Boston isn't much fun."

"I understand why you bought a house. I understand why you want to get rid of the one you're in—never understood how you could spend another night there after what happened." All said carefully. "But let's look at the chain of events and how underlying emotional issues set you up for something you don't want to repeat. Ever."

She looks around, making sure no one is listening, looks out at the rain, at gaslights and slick cobblestones, her face touched by sadness for an instant.

"Your father died last year," Win continues in a quiet voice, leaning into their conversation, elbows on the white tablecloth. "Left half of everything to you. Not that you were hurting before, but now you have what most people would consider a fortune. Still doesn't account for your subsequent behavior. You've never been a have-not. So for you to become a wild, crazy spender means something else is going on. Hundreds of thousands of dollars on clothing, a car, who knows what else, all cash. Millions on a house when you already own a multimillion-dollar house, and you rent a place at the Ritz. Cash, more cash, all this cash moving from a French bank to a Boston bank, to who knows how many banks."

"My father had accounts in London, Los Angeles, New York, Paris, Switzerland. How else do you move large sums of cash if not by wire transfers? Most people don't use suitcases. And paying cash for clothing, for automobiles, is what I've always done. Never buy things on credit that begin to depreciate the minute you leave the store. As for the house on Brattle? In this dreadful market, I got it for a song compared to what it will be worth after I fix it up—if and when the day ever comes that our economy recovers. I didn't need a mortgage for deductions, and I really don't care to discuss the nuances of my financial portfolio with you."

"In point of fact. You moved huge amounts of money. Made huge purchases in cash. Went on a spending spree the likes of which I've never seen with you, and I've known you for a fairly long time. Donated to charities you didn't check out. Then you get involved with . . ."

"No names." She holds up her hand.

"Certainly convenient to own a house you don't live in and isn't in your name," Win says. "Good place to have a meeting or two. Or three or four. Bad idea to have such meetings at the Ritz. Or a house where the neighbors know you and maybe watch you out their windows. Not good to have meetings in college housing." Drinks his wine. "With a college kid." Holds up his glass. "This is pretty good."

She looks away from him. "What's going to come out in court?"

"Hard to imagine he's a juvenile. I wouldn't have guessed."

"He lied."

"You didn't check."

"Why would I?"

"You ever notice needle marks on his hands, speaking of not checking things? Fingertips, palms."

"Yes."

"You ask him?"

"Botox injections so his hands wouldn't sweat," she says. "His father's a plastic surgeon. You know that. Started giving them to him when he was performing. You know, piano recitals. So his fingers didn't slip on the keys. Now he continues the Botox because he plays keyboard, is used to it."

"And you believed that."

"Why wouldn't I?"

"I suppose," Win says. "Can't say it would enter my mind, either. Unless I were already suspicious of the person. Not to mention, I've never heard of anybody doing that. Botox in their fingertips. Must hurt like hell."

"Wouldn't be foolproof," Lamont says.

"Nothing is. But you walk into a bank, shove a note under the glass, and your hands are clean and dry. No prints on paper."

"Good luck proving all this."

"We have his copper print, for lack of a better thing to call it. On the camera box he stupidly left in the kitchen of your new-old house. Don't worry. He's going to be locked up for quite some time," Win says.

"What's going to happen?"

"I don't understand your question," he says.

She gives him her eyes. "Of course you do."

The waiter wanders toward them, picks up her signal, and retreats.

"He's a pathological liar," Win says. "The one time there was a meeting that was witnessed by others? Well, not only was he not there but the witnesses are aware of a sting operation that explains various electronic communications that frankly the Feds and others might prefer the public didn't know about. Since the Patriot Act is about as popular as the bubonic plague."

"You were there before," she says. "At the house. And saw me return to my car. And what I was carrying. And all the rest."

"No evidence of that, and I never saw him that night. I will say, however, I don't appreciate someone wearing my skin. Part of the thrill. Stealing my stuff . . ."

"Setting you up?"

"No. Stealing me. Psychological," Win says. "Probably goes back to what his mother said about me when they were apartment shopping, which had to make him feel more inadequate and resentful than he already felt. Anyway. I guess in his own way, he put on my skin, walked around in my shoes. Overpowered me in his own weirdo way. You didn't drink the wine he stole from me."

"Wasn't in the mood," she says, giving him her eyes again. "Wasn't in the mood for any of it, to tell the truth. Had gotten out of the mood rather quickly, which didn't set well, if you understand what I mean."

"Boy toy gets boring."

"I would prefer you not make comments like that."

"So on that occasion, the one I sort of witnessed, things didn't go well. When I saw you leave the courthouse, you seemed to be arguing. Were on your cell phone. You seemed upset, and I followed you."

"Yes, arguing. I didn't want to go there. To the house. He was persuasive. Had things on me. Made it difficult for me to refuse. I'll be candid for a moment and tell you I didn't know how I was going to get out of it. And further, I have no idea how I got into it to begin with."

"I'll be candid for a moment and tell you how it all happened. In my opinion," he says. "When we feel powerless, we do things that make us feel powerful. Our appearance. Our clothing. Our homes. Our cars. Pay cash. Do whatever we can to feel desirable. Sexy. Including, well, maybe even exhibitionism." He pauses. "Let me guess. He made those YouTube videos. But it wasn't his idea, it was yours. One more thing he had on you."

Her silence is her answer.

"Got to give it to you, Monique. I think you're the shrewdest human being I've ever met."

She drinks her wine. "What if he says something about it. To the police. Or worse, in court," Lamont says.

"You mean airs your dirty laundry, so to speak? Which you were smart enough not to leave at the scene after your . . . ?"

"If he says something about anything," she interrupts.

"He's a liar." Win shrugs.

"It's true. He is."

"The other thing when we feel powerless?" Win says. "We pick someone safe."

"Obviously not so. This was anything but safe."

"Want to feel desirable but safe," Win says. "The older, powerful woman. Adored but safe, because she's in control. What could be safer than a bright, artistic boy who follows you like a puppy."

"Do you think Stump's safe?" Lamont says, nodding at the waiter.

"By which you're implying . . . ?"

"I think you know what I'm implying."

She'll have greens with vinaigrette, and a double order of tuna carpaccio with wasabi. He orders his usual steak. A salad. No potato.

"We're close friends," Win says. "Work and play well with each other."

It's obvious Lamont wants to know two things but can't bring herself to ask. Is he in love with Stump, and did she tell him what happened long years ago when Lamont got drunk in Watertown?

"Let me ask again," Lamont says. "Is she safe?"

"Let me tell you again. We're close friends. I feel perfectly safe. How about you?"

"I expect you back in the unit on Monday," Lamont says. "So I'm not sure how much you'll be working with her anymore. Unless, of course, there's a homicide and she rolls up in that rather ridiculous truck. Which brings me to one last point. The organization she started."

"The FRONT."

"What should we do about it?"

"I don't think there's anything we can do about it," Win says. "It's moved in like a front, rather much living up to its name. You're not going to get rid of it."

"I wasn't suggesting any such thing," Lamont says. "I was wondering what we might do to help. If that would please her."

"Please Stump?"

"Yes, her. Keep her happy. And safe."

"If I were you, I would," Win says. "Safe to say, that would be a smart thing to do."

AT RISK

Patricia Cornwell

A Massachusetts state investigator is called home from the National Forensic Academy in Tennessee. His boss, an attractive but hard-charging woman, is running for governor, and as a showcase plans to use a new crime initiative called At Risk – motto: 'Any crime, any time.' She's looking for a way to employ cutting-edge DNA technology, and thinks she's found it in a twenty-year-old murder – in Tennessee. If her office solves the case, they'll all look pretty good, right?

Her investigator is not so sure but before he can open his mouth, a shocking piece of violence intervenes, an act that shakes up not only their lives but the lives of everyone around them . . .

'In *At Risk*, Cornwell has returned to what she does best . . . Superb.' *Independent*

Fiction
978-0-7515-3871-7

POSTMORTEM

Patricia Cornwell

A serial killer is on the loose in Richmond, Virginia. Three women have died, brutalised and strangled in their own bedroom. There is no pattern: the killer appears to strike at random – but always early on Saturday mornings.

So when Dr Kay Scarpetta, chief medical officer, is awakened at 2.33 am, she knows the news is bad: there is a fourth victim. And she fears now for those that will follow unless she can dig up new forensic evidence to aid the police.

But not everyone is pleased to see a woman in this powerful job. Someone may even want to ruin her career and reputation . . .

'Terrific first novel, full of suspense, in which
even the scientific bits grip'
The Times

Fiction
978-0-7515-3043-8

BOOK OF THE DEAD

Patricia Cornwell

The 'book of the dead' is the morgue log, the ledger in which all cases are entered by hand. For Kay Scarpetta, however, it is about to have a new meaning.

Fresh from her bruising battle with a psychopath in Florida, Scarpetta decides it's time for a change of pace. Moving to the historic city of Charleston, South Carolina, she opens a unique private forensic pathology practice, one in which she and her colleagues offer expert crime scene investigation and autopsies to communities lacking local access to competent death investigation and modern technology. It seems like an ideal situation, until the murders and other violent deaths begin.

A woman is ritualistically murdered in her multi-million-dollar beach home. The body of an abused young boy is found dumped in a desolate marsh. A sixteen-year-old tennis star is found nude and mutilated near Piazza Navona in Rome.

Scarpetta has dealt with many brutal and unusual crimes before, but never a string of them as baffling, or as terrifying, as the ones before her now. Before she is through, that book of the dead will contain many names – and the pen may be poised to write her own.

'Patricia Cornwell is the queen of gritty, grisly, crime fiction writing and her latest offering doesn't disappoint. *Book of the Dead* will keep you gripped throughout' *Heat*

Fiction

978-0-7515-4074-1